"I'm not interested in starting something I don't stand a chance of finishing.

"I'll be here for weeks," Max said. "You're going to leave in a couple of days."

Darcy's brow scrunched into that "I'm checking you out" frown, the one that made her bottom lip full and tempting. As if it needed any help. "What makes you think I'm leaving in two days?"

Uh-oh.

Foreboding mingled with an edgy thrill and finally with a ragged fear. This was about more than turning away a woman who was wrong for him. About more than protecting her from tangling her life with a man who wanted nothing from a relationship except sex.

This was about keeping her well away from a situation that could turn deadly in a heartbeat.

Resisting Darcy for a couple of days was tough enough. Resisting those mermaid curves and siren eyes for three weeks straight would be damned near impossible.

And if he screwed up this mission, she could be the one to pay. A hell he vowed never to visit again.

Dear Reader,

Welcome to another month of the most exciting romantic reading around, courtesy of Silhouette Intimate Moments. Starting things off with a bang, we have *To Love a Thief* by ultrapopular Merline Lovelace. This newest CODE NAME: DANGER title takes you back into the supersecret world of the Omega Agency for a dangerous liaison you won't soon forget.

For military romance, Catherine Mann's WINGMEN WARRIORS are the ones to turn to. These uniformed heroes and heroines are irresistible, and once you join Darcy Renshaw and Max Keagan for a few *Private Maneuvers,* you won't even be trying to resist, anyway. Wendy Rosnau continues her unflashed miniseries THE BROTHERHOOD in *Last Man Standing,* while Sharon Mignerey's couple find themselves *In Too Deep.* Finally, welcome two authors who are new to the line but not to readers. Kristen Robinette makes an unforgettable entrance with *In the Arms of a Stranger,* and Ana Leigh offers a matchup between *The Law and Lady Justice.*

I hope you enjoy all six of these terrific novels, and that you'll come back next month for more of the most electrifying romantic reading around.

Enjoy!

Leslie J. Wainger
Executive Editor

Please address questions and book requests to:
Silhouette Reader Service
U.S.: 3010 Walden Ave., P.O. Box 1325, Buffalo, NY 14269
Canadian: P.O. Box 609, Fort Erie, Ont. L2A 5X3

Private
Maneuvers
CATHERINE
MANN

INTIMATE MOMENTS™

Published by Silhouette Books

America's Publisher of Contemporary Romance

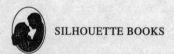 SILHOUETTE BOOKS

ISBN 0-373-27296-0

PRIVATE MANEUVERS

Copyright © 2003 by Catherine Mann

Visit us at www.eHarlequin.com

Printed in U.S.A.

Books by Catherine Mann

Silhouette Intimate Moments

Wedding at White Sands #1158
*Grayson's Surrender #1175
*Taking Cover #1187
*Under Siege #1198
The Cinderella Mission #1202
*Private Maneuvers #1226

*Wingmen Warriors

CATHERINE MANN

writes contemporary military romances, a natural fit since she's married to her very own USAF research source. Prior to publication, Catherine graduated with a B.A. in fine arts: theater from the College of Charleston and received her master's degree in theater from UNC Greensboro. During her college days, she even supported herself with stints as a puppeteer and mime. She has also written for a newspaper, taught on a university level and served as a theater school director. Now happily penning her stories about men and women in uniform, Catherine finds following her aviator husband around the world with four children, a beagle and a tabby in tow offers her endless inspiration for new plots. Learn more about her work, as well as her adventures in military life, by visiting her Web site: http://catherinemann.com. Or contact her at P.O. Box 41433, Dayton, OH 45441.

To my wonderful daughter, Haley, whose dolphin affinity inspired this story. I love you, kiddo!

And to my cousin—Jim Fowler, former navy diving and salvage officer. Thank you for all your help with diving research. And most of all, thanks for the fun memories of summers at Grandma and Graddad's river house. I may have built a better Girl Scout fire, but you always could swim faster. And how about we call that game of Monopoly a draw? Thanks bunches!

Chapter 1

First Lieutenant Darcy "Wren" Renshaw flung her flight checklist on the planning room table with a resounding smack. Not much of an outlet for her frustration, but the satisfying thunk on scarred wood made her feel marginally better.

While her siblings pounded dictators in Southeast Asia, she was stuck flying Flipper to Guam.

Restrained anger pinged inside her like antiaircraft missiles. Darcy spun an empty chair and dropped into the seat at the lengthy conference table, eager to start and therefore finish this mission all the sooner.

For once she didn't plunge into conversation with the other aircrew members plotting their early-morning takeoff from San Diego bound for Guam—an island that still haunted her dreams. No need to infect the crew with her rotten mood. After all, transporting marine biologist Dr. Maxwell Keagan and his two bottlenose dolphins to the South Pacific was considered an honor.

An honor for the rest of the C-17 crew maybe, but for her? Darcy knew better. She hadn't earned this cake mission, an embarrassing reality that burned over her with the devouring speed of flaming jet fuel.

How dare her three-star-general father "encourage" the Squadron Commander to yank Darcy's combat slot to Cantou and schedule her as a last-minute substitute on the safer Flipper Flight? She'd worked her boots off to be deserving of the wings on her leather nametag since the first day of pilot training. She wouldn't start quietly accepting gift-wrapped cushy assignments now.

Sounds of Air Force crewdogs at work wrapped around her, the familiar routine offering none of its usual excitement. Rustling charts, clipped banter. Pilots. Loadmasters. Ground support. Every one of them having already pulled their rotation in conflicts around the world. She couldn't allow them to shoulder all her risks as well as their own.

Once she off-loaded Dr. Dolittle and his dolphin duo in Guam, she would confront her commander. If she wasn't qualified for combat in the Cantou conflict, then he should remove her from flying status altogether.

Darcy yanked a bag of sunflower seeds from the thigh pocket of her flight suit and wrestled open the cellophane. Munching away emotions she refused to let rule her, she cracked shells, slowly, one at a time to restore her calm while waiting for Dr. Keagan to arrive. "Anybody seen the dolphin doc around yet?"

Captain Tanner "Bronco" Bennett, the aircraft

commander, looked up from his chart. "What's your hurry, Wren? He's got another ten minutes."

"Eight," Darcy answered without checking her watch. "To be early is to be on time."

"Cool your jets. He'll get here when he gets here." Bronco reached into the thigh pocket of his flight suit. "Since we're waiting, have I showed everyone the latest pictures of Kathleen and the baby at the zoo?"

"Yes!" the room collectively shouted.

Bronco held his hands up in good-natured surrender. "Hey, just trying to pass time till the guy arrives."

"I'm starting to wonder if you could fit enough pictures in your pocket for that, Captain." Darcy eased her grouse with a quick grin, drumming her fingers impatiently on the gouged wood.

She hadn't met Keagan yet, having only arrived at the San Diego Naval Air Station from her home base in Charleston, South Carolina, the night before. But the guy must have some heavy-duty clout to warrant military transport for his dolphins.

String pullers weren't high on her list of favorite folks, especially today.

This time General Pops had gone too far with the overprotectiveness. Sure, she'd been kidnapped in Guam as a kid. A terrifying experience for her family, and one she still couldn't dwell on for even thirty seconds without dropping her damned sunflower seeds all over the floor. But it was time to get past it.

Darcy cracked seeds one at time to focus her thoughts and calm her pissed-off senses. Maybe the time had come to confront her father, too. If only she didn't have to confront the inevitable worry on his dear craggy face, as well.

Why couldn't her dad understand that by clipping her wings, he'd always denied her the chance to put that week behind her? Her very nature, inherited from seven generations of Renshaw warriors, demanded she fight back. Like the squadron motto on her patch, she would be ready for Anything. Anywhere. Anytime.

She hadn't expected that to include hauling cetaceans across the Pacific.

Darcy jackhammered another salty seed with her molars.

Bronco spun her chair to face him. "Geez, Renshaw. How about I get you some rocks to chew? Wouldn't be half as noisy."

Bronco's linebacker bulk filled his chair as completely as his teasing filled the room. Darcy shrugged off her irritation and slid into the camaraderie with as much ease as zipping her flight suit. Childhood years spent as a squadron mascot while her classmates earned Scout badges had left her with a slew of surrogate big brothers and the ability to hold her own around any military watercooler.

She sprinkled a pile of sunflower seeds on top of the aircraft commander's chart. "Shelling is an art form, boss man. Didn't they teach you old guys anything when you went to pilot training?"

From across the table, Captain Daniel "Crusty" Baker scooped the shells. "We old guys must have been busy inventing the wheel."

"Old guys? Ouch!" Bronco thumped his chest. "Renshaw deals another lethal blow to the ego. My wife would be proud."

Crusty pitched the seeds into his mouth, swiped his hand along his flight suit and grabbed the bag for a second helping.

Darcy snagged it away, irritation creeping through in spite of her resolve. "Get your own, moocher."

Bronco eased back his chair, a big-brother concern glinting in his eyes she recognized too well. "What's got your G-suit in a knot today, Renshaw?"

Uh-uh. She wasn't answering that one. Her feelings were her own. Always had been since the terrorist raid on her childhood overseas home.

She clenched her fist around the shells until they sliced into her palm. One rogue seed spurted between her fingers and spiraled to the carpet. She inched her flight boot over it to conceal the seed as well as her momentary lapse.

Darcy popped another seed into her mouth. "I'm sorry. Were you talking?" She scavenged a quick grin. "I couldn't hear you over my crunching."

Chuckling, the two senior captains resumed pouring over Bronco's chart.

Tipping back her seat, Darcy dragged the industrial-size trash can forward and pitched her hulls inside. Time to launch this flight and bring her closer to launching her life, as well. She rolled her chair away from the table. "I'm going to find out what's keeping Keagan so we can get this mission off the ground."

Footsteps sounded from the hall, stalling Darcy half standing. The door swung open, voices swelling through as three men strode in, two in naval khaki uniforms, one in creased pants and a bow tie.

Ah, the professor.

Just as Darcy started to look away, another man strolled through the doorway. One glimpse at him and she lost all interest in studying flight data scrawled on the dry erase board.

Holy marine mammal, the guy was hot.

Six foot two, three maybe. Early thirties? Given his laid-back air and casual clothes, perhaps he was the graduate assistant accompanying the professor on the flight. A graduate assistant who looked as if he spent all his after-school hours on a surfboard.

Sandy-brown hair spiked from his head, the tips bleached from overexposure to the sun. The damp disarray could have been styled deliberately, but somehow she didn't think so. His five-o'-clock shadow at 8:00 a.m. hinted his only comb might be fingers tunneling through sun-kissed hair.

A sea-foam-colored windbreaker was zipped halfway up his broad chest. The banded waist grazed the top of his low-riding drawstring swim trunks. Slim hips and an incredible tush were covered by…flowers.

Loud tangerine and purple blooms blazoned from faded nylon hitting right around knee-length, obliterating her earlier frustration in a Technicolor sensory tidal wave.

After hanging out in an almost exclusively male world all her life, she wasn't often rattled by a man's physical appearance. So why were her fingers itching to comb through this guy's hair?

The senior Navy officer paused beside the dry erase board. "Sorry for the delay. Ladies and gentlemen, let me introduce Dr. Maxwell Keagan, head of Marine Mammal Communications at the University of San Diego. And his research assistant, Perry Griffin. Now that they've arrived, I'll set up the computer and projector while you introduce yourselves." The officer turned to the two civilians. "Dr. Keagan, we'll be ready for your brief in about five minutes."

"Thank you, Commander."

Huh?

Dr. Keagan's answer hadn't come from Mr. Bow Tie, but from the surfboarder dude with incredible pecs and horrid fashion sense.

Darcy dropped into her seat with more force than a botched parasail landing. She blinked, stared again.

Sure enough those tropical-flower-clad hips were advancing toward her end of the table for an introduction. Not Mr. Bow Tie. That guy was crawling along the floorboards searching for an outlet for the computer like an eager-to-please research assistant.

Surfboarder dude extended his hand. "Dr. Max Keagan."

A beach bum with a brain. Fantasies didn't come any better.

"Hello, Doctor." Standing, she transferred her sunflower seeds to her left hand and extended her right. "Lieutenant Darcy Renshaw."

His callused fingers enfolded hers, his scent chasing right up the link to blanket her with intoxicating potency. Coconut oil, salty air and a hint of musk wafted from him, like a piña colada after long, sweaty sex on the beach.

If she'd ever had such a moment.

For a crazy, impulsive second, Darcy wondered what it would be like to make that memory—with this guy. A shiver whispered through her that had nothing to do with the *whoosh* of the air conditioner.

Did she see an answering attraction in his blue-green eyes? Maybe the slightest narrowing of his gaze to one of those sleepy-lidded assessments she'd seen her eight kazillion pseudo big brothers give other women when—

Bronco cleared his throat just before the chair behind Darcy jarred the back of her knees. Damn. Did the big guy have to kick it so hard? Be so obvious in pointing out she was still clasping Max Keagan's fingers?

Darcy jerked her hand away and glanced over her shoulder. Sure enough, the pilots stood side by side, a mismatched Mutt and Jeff with identical smirks.

Double damn and dirt. They would razz the hell out of her all the way across the Pacific.

She willed herself not to blush. Salvaging what she could of her pride and professionalism, Darcy pulled to attention. "Dr. Keagan, a pleasure to meet you."

Pleasure? She stifled a groan at her word choice.

Bronco snorted.

Forget salvaging squat. She turned on her boot heel toward the aircraft commander. "With all due respect, sir, I'm going to roll you off the load ramp right after we cross into international airspace."

She faced Max Keagan again, unable to read anything on the man's tanned—gorgeous—face. "I apologize for him and for my, uh…" Adolescent drooling? Mortifying lack of self-control? "For staring. You aren't quite what I expected."

"No problem. I've heard the same in more than one faculty meeting." He let her off the hook with a few simple words.

Oh, man. Smart, hunky and nice enough to grant her an easy reprieve when he could have been an egotistical jerk.

She was toast.

"Let's start again." Composure thankfully back in place, Darcy made the formal introductions without a hitch. They settled into their chairs, Bronco and Crusty suddenly opting for a new seating chart that left only one place for Dr. Keagan. Next to Darcy.

Great. Now instead of teasing her, they were "helping.'' She had her very own hulking Cupid with a sunflower-mooching cohort.

She probably needed their help. And then some.

If only she possessed as much ease with flirting as she did with touch-and-go landings.

Touch-and-go. Her heart rate fired like jet pistons chugging to life. Why did a routine flight term suddenly sound sexy courtesy of Dr. Keagan?

Duh! Because his bad-boy, fine self was sitting no less than eighteen inches away, his eyes gliding over her flight suit with a heat she'd never, never had sizzle her way before from any guy. After all, men did not look at their best bud that way, even if said bud was a woman.

Darcy savored the heat all the way to her toes.

Twenty-five years of virginity, of overprotective relatives, of being everybody's pal and never the object of those sleepy-lidded stares, weighed her down like a seventy-pound survival pack ready to be shed after a marathon trek. She was tired of being slotted into safer roles.

Why wait until after this mission to go for what she wanted? Here was a big, hunky risk ready for the taking.

And she could have that risk without breaking her personal rule. No military men. No men like her father, government protectors by training, trade and blood.

Before she lost her nerve, Darcy extended her fist toward Max. Her fingers unfurled to reveal a now-steady palm full of sunflower seeds. ''Want some?''

Max stared at that slim hand, up to Darcy Renshaw's wrist where a pulse double-timed in a fragile vein.

He wanted a lot more than sunflower seeds from the leggy dynamo seated beside him. Her flight suit and take-no-lip attitude assured him she could probably down the average man in five different ways. One helluva woman, no doubt.

Not that he intended to act on the impulse to accept that challenge. Following impulses could get even the best of CIA officers killed.

Or worse yet, someone else.

"Thanks. But I'll pass."

A flicker of disappointment chased through her amber-brown eyes. Followed by an impish flash of determination.

Well, damn. Flattering, sure, but her timing stunk. He couldn't afford distractions, not now when eighteen months of deep cover was about to pay off.

Finally he would discover the traitor who'd sold out Eva two and a half years ago.

Captain Baker's arm shot past toward the seeds. "I'll take 'em, Wren."

She blasted him with an exasperated eye roll. "Crusty, do you ever get full?"

"Nope. My jaws just get tired of chewing." The wiry relief pilot grinned.

The other pilot added his nod of agreement.

In need of mental distancing from the leggy distraction beside him, Max studied the three bickering crew members who would fly him across the Pacific. He slid into work mode with determined focus, mentally merging the real people with the profiles from his intelligence briefing.

Captain Tanner "Bronco" Bennett. Air Force Academy grad who'd turned down a seven-figure pro-football contract to serve his country. Combat vet. Trustworthy, team player down the line.

A dry smile tugged at Max. His father would have given his favorite fishing pole to have a son like that.

Too bad, old man. You got me.

Max shifted to the next pilot. Captain Daniel "Crusty" Baker. That rumpled flight suit housed a razor-sharp liaison to the Air Force's Office of Special Investigations. A dark-ops test pilot with a penchant for junk food—and the only one on the crew who knew Max's real mission. As much as Max chafed at checking in with anyone, he accepted the military intel contact as necessary if he wanted this operation. And he did. Badly.

He allowed his gaze to stray to the last flyer. The one he'd forced himself not to assess first simply because he wanted to look at her too much.

First Lieutenant Darcy "Wren" Renshaw. Military brat with an impressive Air Force family tree. Top graduate out of ROTC and pilot training. And Papa's pampered princess, slotted as a last-minute sub on a primo mission.

Max let his gaze linger.

Darcy shot repeated comebacks to her crew while scooping a hand into her thigh pocket. He had to admit. Those were great thighs attached to her sleek body.

She tugged out her blue military hat, then dug deeper. As she reached, he studied the back of her head, the silky cap of short brown hair.

No, wait. Brown wasn't the exact color and details were important in his job. Right?

He looked again, resisting the urge to test the texture with his fingers. Cinnamon, maybe? Like the stuff a neighbor lady of his used to sprinkle on golden-brown cookies warm from the oven.

Darcy whipped out another bag of sunflower seeds and pitched them across the room, catching Crusty Baker square in the chest. "That's it, Baker. No more mooching or I'll tell the flight kitchen to fill your lunch with raw eggs."

She turned her back on the two pilots, her full attention on Max. "Must be pretty cool wearing a swimsuit to work."

"Saves on dry cleaning." Max flipped a mental switch, shutting off all thoughts except his upcoming crew brief.

Darcy propped her elbow on the table, chin on her palm, landing smack in Max's line of sight. "So you spend a lot of hands-on time with your job?"

Hands-on? With two little words, she'd flipped that switch right back.

He told his libido to take a swan dive off the nearest cliff. "With applied science labs at the university—" along with marine mammal training at the Pt. Loma, California, naval facility "—I spend the majority of my time in the water."

Which was true. Two cardinal rules of undercover work: keep it close to the truth; keep it simple. And a small uncorrupted part of himself resisted lying to an innocent.

Better drown that impulse, too, chump.

"Ever been to Guam before?"

Damn, but she was nosy underneath all that guileless enthusiasm.

He rolled out his rehearsed cover story that mixed in a splash of truth. "I went to the South Pacific a few years ago while writing my dissertation.'' Truth, minus the part that the CIA had already recruited him. He'd annotated footnotes while dodging bullets in some Southeast Asian cesspool. ''I was part of the dolphin rescue team flown out when two calves beached in Guam.''

''Now you're the one to set them free. How cool to get closure.'' She edged forward, her scent of baby powder and soap edging further right into his senses.

''Guess you could call it that.'' God, she smelled good. Clean and untainted, and so unlike anything he'd been exposed to in years. He'd almost forgotten people like her existed, were in fact the very reason he'd signed on with the CIA. Back in a time when he'd planned to save the world and have the secret satisfaction of showing up his father.

See, Old Man, I can serve my country as well as you, but on my own terms. Screw creased uniforms and buzz cuts.

Max nudged a stray sunflower seed with his foot. His ratty deck shoes made an appropriate contrast to the polished sheen of Renshaw's combat boots.

''So, Doc, did you always want to work with dolphins? Be a marine biologist?''

Time to turn those questions around. ''Did you always want to join the Air Force?''

''Yes,'' she said.

But her eyes said no.

An awkward silence settled.

He studied her suddenly guarded eyes and wondered at the reason. She seemed one hundred percent military. Crisp conformity and camaraderie above all.

He knew the type well, just like his old man. The Air Force uniform on the C-17 crew might differ from his father's Navy whites, but Max recognized the military mantle that transcended service branches. All the same, he felt those glimmering eyes luring him like a mythological siren.

Not wise on the job.

Max forced himself to remember every detail of Eva's murder. How he'd been unable to save his lover, his CIA dive partner. How he'd held her in the crashing surf while she bled out. Taking their unborn child with her. All because some faceless bastard had been turning over American agents in the Pacific.

No way in hell would Max lose this chance to put a name to that traitor. Finally he'd found the link when the military reported intercepted communications. Agency intel analysis pointed to a leak in Guam, most likely a tap on one of the military's oceanic communications cables.

Time was critical now with missions being flown in the Cantou conflict. Intercepted flight-planning data could allow the enemy to shoot down U.S. aircraft at will.

Shutting down all underwater cables out of the island wasn't an option. But once he identified the tapped cable with the help of his trained dolphins, a few tantalizing nuggets of transmitted misinformation would bait the trap. Then the CIA would tighten the net around the whole enemy spy ring.

Tighten around one double agent in particular, and by God, Max wouldn't let anything distract him from being the one to reel that traitor in.

A flash from the projector jarred Max back to the present. The Navy officer dimmed the lights to half power. "All set. Dr. Keagan, are you ready to begin?"

"Of course." Max shoved out of his chair. Hell yes, he was ready to lose himself in work.

Turning from the lure of siren eyes, Max focused on his graphs projected onto the screen. He worked better as a loner anyway, always had.

The less a man had, the less he had to lose.

This time, Max Keagan will lose it all.

The operative known as Robin stood on a rocky outcropping and scanned the Pacific skyline. Soon Max would be in Guam. A fitting place to finish it since the South Pacific island carried so much history for both of them.

The rest of the world might buy that sappy cover story about freeing a couple of dolphins, but Robin knew better. Sure they would be set free. Eventually. But first the trained government dolphins would perform one last mission with CIA Officer Maxwell Keagan.

Together they would locate the tap the Cantou government had placed on a U.S. military underwater communications cable.

A mission Keagan could not be allowed to accomplish. Too much valuable information filtered through that line.

The phone vibrated in Robin's hand with an incoming call. Encrypted cell phones made this too easy. "Yeah?"

"We expected an update yesterday."

"I'm on it. Keagan takes off before sunrise." Waves crashed against the rocky cliff. Salty spray stung the skin, the eyes, rasping against every sense and demanding remembrance of another time.

"Do you need more support?"

"Negative." Definitely not. No one else would get a shot at Max. Personal debts demanded payment face-to-face. "Give me time to monitor his underwater search pattern."

"Good point. With any luck he'll be miles off. As long as he and his dolphins aren't close to the transmitter, there's no need to risk riling the Agency by eliminating him."

Robin stifled the urge to argue. Not a chance would Keagan walk away. Max would die this time, even if it meant feeding him enough information to put him and his godawful flamboyant wet suits on top of that line tap.

If only it were as simple as just popping him. But without the payoff, there would be no plush retirement.

No. Better to make Keagan's death palatable to the other side. "I'll check back when I have more."

Robin disconnected. Anticipation stung with as much power as the exploding surf.

Only a few weeks at the most until the easy life in Switzerland, thanks to money saved from years of bartering secrets to other countries. Ensuring the security on that tap of the U.S. military's oceanic communications cable out of Guam would rake in the final jackpot.

Not to mention an added bonus in the sweetest payoff of all—finally delivering lethal revenge to Maxwell Keagan.

And heaven help anyone who stood in the way.

Chapter 2

"Would you *please* get out of my way?" Darcy elbowed aside Crusty's arm before he could swipe her sunflower seeds from the C-17's control panel. "In case you haven't noticed, I'm trying to fly an airplane."

"Show some respect for your elders." Crusty's chuckling voice echoed through the headset from his seat behind her.

"Yeah, yeah." She pitched the bag over her shoulder while keeping her other hand steady on the stick.

The night sky swam before her windscreen. Stars dotted the panorama as if dropped there, like in one of her nephew's pop-up books. Bronco sprawled in the aircraft commander's seat beside her, reading a book and periodically checking her controls.

All in all, a great night for flying.

She glanced at the HUD, Heads-Up Display. The plexiglass screen at eye level mirrored the instrument panel so she never had to take her eyes off the sky. Not that there was much to see in the inky darkness, but a night flight had been crucial for temperature control for the dolphins.

Dolphins. Max Keagan.

Double damn and dirt.

One simple thought about the unusual freight blew her concentration. Her attention winged straight back to the cargo hold of dolphins and their spiky-haired trainer.

"Think about flying," she whispered, chanting, "charts, airspeed, whiz wheels, flight times."

The 4:00 a.m. takeoff from coastal San Diego would keep them in the dark as they chased time zones west. Even with their twelve hours in the air, the sun would only just be rising in Guam once they landed.

Then she wouldn't have the distractions of instrumentation checks and flight schedules to keep her thoughts from lofting along tempting routes. Sure the dolphin doctor's eyes had blazed interest initially. Until his brief. Then she might as well have been stuck behind a Vulcan cloaking device for all the notice he took of her.

Darcy sighed and wondered why the usual spice of flying seemed flat tonight, like unsalted sunflower seeds. She lived for these moments in the air. She'd fought a major battle with her father over entering pilot training.

Of course Pops had won big-time this week by keeping her out of any real war. Irritation tightened her grip on the stick.

Bronco shut his book. "Have I showed you the latest pictures of Kathleen and the baby at the beach?"

"Yes!" Darcy and Crusty said. The headset echoed with the loadmaster's affirmative from the back.

"Oh." Bronco deflated like a parachute deprived of wind.

Darcy flipped the autopilot switch and wriggled her fingers for the pictures. "But I'd love to see them again."

A smile wreathed Bronco's big mug as he passed the pack. "Just for that, my now favorite copilot, you get the takeoff when we leave Guam, while ol' Crusty there warms that jump seat again."

Anticipation fired through her. A takeoff was a rare thrill for any copilot. Training requirements called for copilots to log more landings than takeoffs. Which logistically made sense because the aircraft commander would always be on hand for takeoff, but a copilot needed to be prepared to land if the senior pilot became incapacitated. Or was shot in combat.

The possibility of an imminent war-zone assignment clenched inside her as tightly as her white-knuckled fist on the beach pictures. Not that she was afraid, she told herself. No way. A Renshaw showed no fear. She wanted a chance to make a difference in Cantou like her bomber navigator brother and fighter pilot sister. They didn't have to battle their dad for every walk on the edge the way Darcy did.

She needed this chance to reconcile her past.

All the more reason to look forward to that takeoff from Guam. Except, when she left, she would say goodbye to the aloof professor.

Her sweaty palms stuck to the pictures.

Bronco jabbed a beefy finger toward an image of an infant wearing a sunbonnet by the ocean. "That's Tara taking her first swim."

Darcy loosened her hold on the photos before she crimped the edges. The fella looked so darn proud, she didn't dare pick at him for stating the obvious. "Cool. Maybe you can sign her up for one of those baby swimming classes."

"Already on the schedule at the base pool."

"I'll be waiting for the pictures." She thumbed through the stack with one hand. No landmark occasion recorded. Just twenty-four near-identical shots of a redheaded mother sitting on a beach towel with a chubby baby.

Nothing much, but somehow it pricked at Darcy, revealing an emptiness she didn't dare call loneliness. Since she never allowed relationships into the workplace and she always worked, her social life sucked. Which meant she would just have to live with that emptiness and get on with her job.

Or maybe not.

Her memory filled with that momentary flash of interest in Max Keagan's eyes. Okay, so he'd backed off once he'd stepped up to brief the crew, but damn it, she hadn't misread the attraction she'd seen.

Hell, barely twenty-four hours after her great resolve for going after what she wanted and already she'd surrendered at the first sign of resistance. She wasn't looking to make her own pack of Kodak memories with the guy, not at the expense of losing focus on her career. She just wanted something to fill that lonely corner of herself. A relationship with a man that went beyond big-brother teasing, if only for the duration of her stay in Guam.

Step it up, soldier. Winners never quit and quitters never win. Time for a jaunt to the cargo hold.

Darcy tucked the pictures into the envelope.

"Crusty, are you sick of that jump seat yet? I need to stretch my legs."

Bronco tapped his headset. "Hey, Crusty, is this thing working right? I could have sworn I heard Wren give up the stick. Voluntarily."

"Yeah, man. I heard the same thing. Too bad we don't have a doc on board to check her temp— Hey wait, Bronco." Crusty gasped in mock surprise. "We *do* have a doctor on board."

"Imagine that," Bronco answered. "Do you think that's why she needs a little stroll in back?"

"You are a genius, my friend."

"Seems we have some private maneuvers already in action on this mission."

Darcy vowed to sabotage their flight lunches.

Except she knew they only teased people they liked. Great. Lucky for her, apparently she really was their favorite copilot.

"Funny, guys. With lame jokes like that, you should take your show on the road." Darcy flipped the auto pilot switch off. "Bronco, do you have the jet?"

The stick waggled in her hand just before Bronco answered. "Roger, I have the jet."

Crusty groused, "Can't believe she called our jokes lame, Bronco."

"Well there aren't privates in the Air Force. Just airmen."

"Details, details…"

She whipped off her headset and unstrapped from the copilot seat. Double-timing, she descended the narrow stairwell into the cargo hold before the pilots could razz her again. The cavernous belly swelled with the tinny echo of activity and engine drones. A red glow hovered throughout, the low lighting set to calm the dolphins during flight. Temperatures had been lowered, as well, per the good doc's instructions.

Scanning for Max, she rubbed her hands along her arms to ward off the chill but found no sign of him in the dimly lit craft. Her stomach lurched with anticipation as it hadn't done since her early days in flight training.

Two rectangular fiberglass tanks lined the center like train carts. The briefings she'd received provided a mental picture of what filled them. A dolphin lay in each one, cradled in a mesh sling. Around ten or eleven feet long, each dolphin rested partially submerged in water.

By the tank farthest from her, the professor's assistant stood beside the loadmaster. Master Sergeant Jim "Tag" Price passed a walk-around oxygen bottle to the assistant. Darcy wasn't fooled by Tag's smile. The seasoned loadmaster ran a tight ship in back and didn't take well to having his rules ignored.

The dolphins were in safe hands. So where was Max?

Bracing a hand along the cool fiberglass, she strode toward Tag. A burst of air whooshed from the dolphin's blowhole. Startled, Darcy jumped, looked around.

Her gaze traveled up until she found Max on the edge of the tank spraying a mist inside. With smooth agility, he swung a leg over, straddling the wall, muscles flexing as he steadied himself.

Rubber boots covered up to his knee, but his toned thigh stayed in plain sight. God, that leg looked good encased in well-worn denim. If she walked a few steps forward and reached up, just a bit…

Darcy hooked her hands on her hips before they turned traitor. Her eyes, however, she allowed free rein to rove before he noticed she'd joined him.

A yellow slicker masked most of Max's chest, protecting him from the backspray. She detected a hint of chambray shirt peeking through the unbuttoned coat.

His rebellious hair spiked, calling her hands to bring on the finger comb. Not that she would with a cargo hold full of people watching. But what *should* she do? Her experience ranked somewhere between nil and nonexistent, unlike her confident older sister.

Maybe that was it.

She would just think like Alicia. Act like Alicia, who'd moved from being president of her senior class to the cockpit of an F-15 in less than a decade.

Being a virgin with next to no experience in the flirting arena didn't mean Darcy hadn't seen others in action. How hard could it be to lift a few of her sister's simpler moves?

Preflighting her plan with a hefty dose of bravado, Darcy braced her shoulders and launched phase two of Operation Dolphin Doc.

"Is it okay for me to be close like this?"

Darcy's husky words punched the air from Max as effectively as a surprise swipe from a powerful dolphin tail. He closed the valve on the hose and looked down into the belly of the cargo plane. "Say again?"

Strolling toward him, she trailed her fingers along the fiberglass tank. "I wouldn't want to upset them by standing too close."

Close to the *dolphins.* Max swallowed a laugh at himself. Damn, but he was so used to looking for hid-

den agendas in undercover assignments he'd missed
the obvious.

Accepting words and a person at face value.

Max hefted himself over the edge of the transport
tank and to the ground, gaining his footing not more
than a few inches from her. Darcy Renshaw was a
rarity. A good, honest person. He didn't doubt his as-
sessment for a second. He'd seen enough corruption-
working CIA ops to recognize innocence.

His own thoughts were far from innocent as he
wondered what it would be like to drag down the zipper on Darcy's flight suit. To reveal every inch of
what waited hidden beneath that bulky green uniform.

He patted the side of the dolphin tank instead to
keep his hands occupied. "You're fine standing where
you are. Sorry if she startled you."

"I thought you said she would sleep for most of
the flight. If so, that's quite a snore she's got going."

"She's just breathing." While he was doing his
damnedest not to breathe in the Darcy-scent of baby
powder and soap mixed with a hint of hydraulic fluid.

"Well, that's a hefty exhale." Darcy scratched a
hand along her collarbone, drawing his attention
straight to that zipper and the translucent skin on her
neck.

Time to roll out some boring academia to send her
sprinting back up to the cockpit. "Dolphins exhale at
over a hundred miles per hour."

She stepped closer. Red fluorescent lights lined the
ceiling of the aircraft, haloing her in sinful enticement.
"It's amazing the force doesn't wake her up."

An air pocket bucked the plane, jostling Darcy
closer still. Max yearned for a bigger plane. "Actu-

ally, dolphins only sleep with one side of the brain at a time.''

''Is it some kind of protection thing? To keep watch for predators? Sharks maybe.''

Renshaw wasn't easily daunted. Okay, he needed to dig deeper into class lectures. ''Dolphins breathe with voluntary muscles. Not like us where it's involuntary. One side of a dolphin's brain always stays awake to regulate breathing.''

''Oh. Kind of like Crusty, huh? Half there sometimes.''

He forced himself to grin back at her mistaken perception about the OSI contact currently sitting in the cockpit. Max had never worried overmuch about the lies inherent in his job before. A means to a better end. Why did it bother him now?

Shake it off and get to work. ''Did you need something?''

''Not really.'' Her whiskey-rich voice mingled with the roar of engines. ''Just taking a break to stretch my legs.''

Legs.

Max kept his famished eyes off those mile-long legs and searched for something safe to study, like her flight suit patches. She shifted from boot to boot, relaying restless nerves at odds with all that gutsy confidence.

A restlessness that inched her so close he could read the stitched lettering on her patches. Her arm declared her squadron's motto of Anything. Anywhere. Anytime.

With her soft-scented body a reach away, the words curled through his brain with shades of meaning he didn't want or need now. "Well then, I'll get back to—"

"Are they both girls?" Darcy pointed to the other transport crate. "Or is that one a boy?"

The woman had a knack with questions, and for a man used to being the one who excavated answers, the experience set him on edge. "Females, both of them."

"What're their names?"

"Lucy and Ethel."

"Lucy and Ethel? And?" Darcy waved a hand for him to continue. "Spill it. There's got to be a story there."

So many people wanted to talk about themselves, he never had trouble keeping his own life closed away by asking the questions. Few pushed past his lifelong reserve.

Certainly no one since Eva.

Max forced his breathing to stay even. "I liked old sitcoms as a kid. *Lost in Space. Gilligan's Island. I Love Lucy.*" Enough about him. Time to turn it around. "What was your favorite show as a kid?"

"*Hogan's Heroes,* of course. While Dad was stationed overseas, we could only get old sitcoms on the base network." Her eyes clouded and she studied her boots until Lucy shooshed again. Darcy's head popped up, her ready smile crinkling her nose again. "But we're not talking about me. Come on. Don't stop now. Why did you settle on Lucy and Ethel rather than, oh, maybe Ginger and Mary Ann or Judy and Penny Robinson?"

Max considered shutting her down with a curt response but couldn't bring himself to douse the animated twinkle in her eyes.

What would it hurt to answer a question that had no bearing on his mission? She would be returning to her home base in days, anyway. "Lucy had this loud cry that made me think of those Lucy tears. You know, that wide-open-mouth cry." He palmed the fiberglass side. "She's temperamental, but she's affectionate. Ethel is the practical one."

He glanced down the belly of the plane where his assistant sprayed the other dolphin. Perry enjoyed disguises, the bow tie being his latest inspiration. Not a field agent, just CIA support personnel adding technical expertise, Perry helped with medical maintenance and setting up the physical environment for the dolphins.

A damned important job, especially with the dolphins' impending release after they completed the underwater search. Max pinched the bridge of his nose absently.

Darcy's eyes narrowed. "Hmm."

"Hmm what?"

"You're frowning."

"I'm concentrating." Or trying to, anyway.

"It's not that kind of frown."

"Frowns come in types?"

"Sure they do. You study nuances of communication, don't you?" Her body language left no room for misunderstanding as she twirled a lock of her hair. "Well, there are definite nuances to frowns. There's the mad frown. Furrows in the brow dropping low over the eyes. Mouth drawn tight."

Darcy demonstrated with an enticing dichotomy of naiveté meets femme fatale. She circled her lips with her finger until Max ached to replace that finger with his own mouth.

Lowering her hand, Darcy pointed across the plane. "Tag over there's giving your assistant one of those frowns right now for almost bumping the load-ramp controls."

Uninterested in looking at Perry or Tag, Max folded his arms over his chest and let her talk. Not that he seemed to have much of a chance of stopping her, anyway. "Okay, I'll buy into that one. What about other frowns?"

"Then there's the megaworried frown. Long furrows on the brow. Jaw thrust forward just a bit." She scrunched her face into a scowl, this time forgoing the attention to her lips, thank God. "The frown my dad gave me this one particular time right before I headed out the door."

"Been there. Seen that one on my old man's face enough times during my teenage years."

"I was twenty-two."

"Hell, Lieutenant," Max said, welcoming the distraction from full lips and flight-suit zippers. "Where were you going? Mars?"

"Pilot training."

There was a story there, no doubt, and he didn't want to hear it. Hearing it would bring her closer, make her more real. Not smart, chump. "All right, we've got the mad frown." Max counted one and two with his fingers. "And the worried frown."

"There's another one."

His instincts blared a warning. Ambush ahead. "Another one?"

She nodded slowly, then hesitated until he thought she might not answer after all. Finally her eyes gleamed with a battlefield determination Max suspected she'd inherited from her old man.

"An interested frown," she continued. "The kind you give someone when you're checking them out but you're not quite sure what to think yet. The forehead still furrows, brows pull together. Head tilts to the side. The mouth isn't tight this time. It's more relaxed."

Darcy lifted a finger to her lips, not quite touching, and swirled the air around them again. She wore that checking-out frown long after her hand fell away. Well beyond the time needed for a simple demonstration.

Max prayed for air. Breathing became a damned near impossible task. He might as well have been one of his dolphins, forced to regulate every pocket of oxygen entering and leaving his body.

He was totally turned on and she hadn't even touched him.

Then her face cleared, forehead smoothed, lips moved. He made himself listen.

"You were wearing that second frown when you looked at Lucy. The overprotective-dad kind of frown when he's worried about sending his kid out." Her brown eyes hinted at a concern far more dangerous than the "interested frown."

The woman was perceptive. And nosy. And he was letting too much show.

Max pivoted toward the tank under the guise of securing a tie-down chain. "It's a tricky transition for dolphins."

"I'll bet you're going to miss them."

"Miss them?" A Navy brat, he'd said hundreds of goodbyes. Pack up and move on. He'd learned early to shrug off the past, to blend into a new setting quickly but never grow attached. Hell, he'd been training for transitory undercover work since the playpen. "It's time for them to go."

The words sounded harsh even to his own jaded ears, but better for her to meet the real Max straight up. He was feeding her enough half-truths about himself. He didn't need to pretend in this arena.

"How will you set them free? What's the process? I did some cruising on the Web when I received this assignment. Most sites said it's tough to reacclimate a dolphin that's been in captivity more than three years."

He grasped the safer topic with both hands. "That's true, but Lucy and Ethel weren't tank dolphins so we're hoping the transition will be smoother. There are fewer risks of them transmitting infection back into the wild that would harm other cetaceans. Lucy and Ethel have spent their captive years in sea pens— netted-off lagoons and bays."

Open ocean operations.

And they always came back.

He wanted this chance for their release, but his concerns about their adaptation strayed to a different path.

He knew they could hunt and protect themselves. But how would they unlearn years of patterned behavior? Not to mention complete loyalty to him. "It's still an iffy situation, but we're gonna give it a shot."

"Hmm."

"Hmm, what?"

"You're still frowning. Why are you doing this if it bothers you?"

"It's not my choice to make." More truth since the dolphins belonged to the government. His hand slid from the tank to his side.

She shoved away from the bulkhead. With one finger she traced his damp handprint on the fiberglass panel. Slowly. Dipping along each curve. "So you did your research in sea pens. Something about communication?"

He nodded. Watched her finger outline the image of his. Clenched his fist. Swallowed hard. "Uh-huh."

"Lucky for you the Air Force could step in on this one. But then I'll bet you probably have a lot of interaction with the folks at the Pt. Loma naval marine research facility since they're close to the university."

His gaze snapped from her hand to her face. *Danger, Will Robinson! Danger!*

How had they gone from discussing old television shows and overprotective fathers to Pt. Loma, the government home of his dolphin training operation?

The woman had all but seduced him from his job without laying a hand on him. Hell, two more seconds and who knew what she might have him spilling. He had to get her off the subject. Now. No time for finesse.

He opted for the first diversion that came to mind.

Max arranged his expression into that checking-out frown, not at all a difficult proposition. "Wanna go out for a drink tomorrow night?"

Sure.

Darcy winced at her inane reply to Max's invitation earlier.

Even eight hours later as she stood on the flight line at Andersen AFB, Guam, she still wanted to exchange her answer for something…snappier. So much for her grand plan of being like her sister, Alicia. But talking with Max had been interesting, then distracting, and before long she was coming on to him for real, being herself.

Boot propped on the load ramp, she watched Max direct the unloading of Lucy and Ethel. The fiberglass crates moved on rollers toward two flatbed trucks.

Palms rustled in the breeze, the ocean visible just beyond the trees. The morning sun crept over the horizon in a shimmering orange ball, warming an already muggy day. Seduced by the sultry tropical breezes, she could almost forget Guam was the scene of so many bad memories.

Darcy plucked at her grimy flight suit, Max looking too darned fresh. The slicker gone, he'd cuffed his chambray sleeves to work with the loadmasters. He steadied the crate during the crane transfer, muscles straining against his well-worn jeans until her toes curled in her boots.

This sexy, fascinating guy had asked her out and the only answer she'd scrounged up was, *Sure.*

Not, *I'll have to get back to you once I've checked the flight schedule.*

Or something elusive but witty like, *We always gather at the Officers' Club. I'm sure we could find an extra bar stool for you.*

Or even just a mature, straightforward, *That sounds great. How about I meet you at the Officers' Club around seven?*

Nope. She'd gone all shivery like some high schooler standing beside her locker with the quarterback.

Sure.

In the distance, wild boonie dogs howled a mocking salute. Not a great omen for her drink date.

Max pulled a clipboard from Tag's hands and

flipped through the pages, scrawling notations. His pen stopped, hovering on the papers.

He looked up, straight at her, and Darcy forgot all about confrontations with her commander and dreaded calls to her father. For a moment she could have sworn she found an echo of her own confusion in Max's eyes. Not that she actually could have seen it since he stood a good twenty or so yards away.

But, oh, what if she had? The notion teased at her, warming that inexperienced ''sure'' part of her more than the morning sun rising overhead.

Perhaps with all that time spent in the hallowed halls of academia, he might not be as savvy as he looked. His dedication to his job and sea mammals was obvious. What if his social life stunk as much as her own, thanks to work?

Her fling fantasy with a beach-bum, genius lothario morphed into a new scenario. Maybe he was shy.

Confident in his academic realm, but as awkward as she was when it came to relationships. That would explain why he'd suddenly blurted out an invitation after seeming reluctant to talk.

Darcy's flagging confidence upped a notch. She didn't imagine for a minute the guy might actually be a virgin, especially after the slow-simmer looks he'd given her. But maybe, just maybe, she'd found someone she could trust enough to be herself with, dopey ''sure'' sorts of answers and all.

Max passed the clipboard back to Tag, circled to the passenger side of the truck and disappeared inside. Darcy exhaled a proverbial hurricane of pent-up air and energy.

Tomorrow she would find him during a break. If she and Max had a chance to talk more before their drink, she could ditch all the butterflies performing aerial maneuvers in her stomach.

She would prove to herself she wasn't afraid to take risks. Surely she'd only been avoiding them out of deference to her father's feelings. Right?

Not because dreams of a dank cement bunker still slipped past her defenses.

Darcy pressed her fingers to her eyes to swipe away sweat and memories she was beyond ready to erase. She focused her gaze as well as her thoughts on the present. The lumbering flatbed truck turned off the flight line onto the narrow road bordering the ocean.

Maybe rather than Max being a big preliminary risk, she'd found a temporary safe haven before she launched into the biggest risk of her life. Putting the past behind her. A mission more important than even her career.

Chapter 3

If I'd wanted safe, don't you think I'd have opted for another career field?'' Max asked the three military intel contacts standing beneath a palm tree. He kept his voice low, although their conversation would likely be masked by the crashing waterfall a few yards away. A pack of howling boonie dogs added to the jungle symphony of humming insects and rustling branches.

Max stared at the stony faces in front of him and knew he wasn't gaining ground. They were determined to tail his every move, had even been waiting when he'd stepped out of the water.

He draped a T-shirt around his neck and tried a different tack. ''I'll concede the need for checking in with reports, but I can't keep tripping over your people.''

''This isn't negotiable, Keagan.'' Crusty Baker hooked his hands on his hips. With his slack demeanor gone, the dark-ops test pilot's lethal edge gleamed in his eyes. All wrinkled flight suits and sunflower seed snitching aside, he made a helluva military intel contact. "Whether you like it or not, there are more people involved. Others at risk."

"You think I don't know that? That's the reason I want this operation streamlined as much as possible." His thoughts shot straight to Darcy. No way around it, her need-to-know-only status put her in a vulnerable position. Contact with him flat-out put her in danger. "This island is too small with too many unknowns. You need to step back and let me do my job."

The Army CID agent in charge of secured communications twirled a tropical flower between her palms. Not that anyone would recognize her as a lethal spook in her floral muumuu and hoop earrings. "You can send me on my way if you want, buddy boy. I'll happily pack up my encryption equipment and enjoy a vacation in the sun. But you'll find it mighty darned difficult to get those reports home by smoke signals and drumbeats."

"Okay." Max nodded his reluctant concession to the muumuu agent. "You've made your point. You I can understand. But Lurch over there…" He jerked a thumb toward the towering Special Operations pararescueman leaning against a palm tree and eagle-eyeing every nook of the jungle. "He's gotta go. Too conspicuous."

Crusty shook his head. "Package deal. Sorry. He's in charge of physical safety. Checking for tails. Hauling your butt out of the water if things go bad."

"I don't need some baby-sitter bodyguard watching my back." Which was why he preferred to work alone. No one took his risks upon themselves anymore.

He stared out at the bay netted off into a sea pen and scrounged for a way to keep Darcy safe. "Put Lurch on another detail. Like watching the crew."

Crusty's jaw flexed. "Renshaw."

"Bennett and the loadmasters, too, of course."

Crusty snorted like Lucy exhaling.

Max gripped the ends of his T-shirt draped around his neck. "You got a problem?"

"She's really buying into the whole professor gig."

"That's the idea." What should have been an undercover victory fell flat. He should be dancing a damned jig over her acceptance of his fake persona.

Rogue thoughts tempted him.

It wasn't totally false. The professor "gig" required more than a few hours spent in the classroom. His deep cover had necessitated classroom lectures and tests to grade.

Operatives frequently had another area of expertise that offered excuses to be in places a known government employee could never enter. To talk freely with people who would clam up at the first signs of a badge.

Which was the beauty of it. Hiding in plain sight. Like with the muumuu granny operative beside him, who would suspect their accountant, bus driver, dental hygienist—professor—of working for the CIA?

Sure he was partially the doc, but his first loyalty lay with the Agency. And Darcy Renshaw had accepted a drink date from the professor, not the real Max who also worked ops in darker places. Max scratched the scar on his shoulder—a *souvenir* from just such an op.

He'd been diving in a South American port to blow up a submarine purchased on the black market for drug running. After setting the explosives, he'd stumbled on two armed diver guards. That scar served as a tangible reminder of how fast a mission could go bad.

Crusty squinted into the sun. "See if you can tone down the beach-boy charm."

Max couldn't stop himself from asking, "Do you have some prior claim to those sunflower seeds?"

"That's not the point."

Like that mattered. "Do you?"

"No."

"Okay, then."

"Not okay." Crusty slapped a bug on his neck. "Her father will have our asses in one of those dolphin slings if something happens to her."

"Isn't she here because of her father?"

"Hell, no. Our squadron commander doesn't give a damn about politics. Colonel Dawson juggled the schedule to give you his best pilots."

"Good enough, then. Let her do her job. You do yours. I'll do mine." And his included keeping his own hands the hell off her sunflower seeds. "She'll be gone from the island before things heat up."

Heat up? Max shut down those thoughts before they led him into more than a drink with Darcy Renshaw.

Darcy.

Unease prickled the hairs along the back of Max's neck. His instincts upgraded to red alert. He scratched a hand along the thin scar on his shoulder while scouring the perimeter.

Lurch straightened away from his tree. "Check your six o'clock. Incoming. Meeting over."

Max scanned the dense jungle and found—a flash of white.

A white shirt. Worn by Darcy.

Frustration and something else he didn't dare label charged through him. He needed to intercept and divert her before she stumbled on faces she would be better off never seeing together. Somebody had to look out for that woman as long as she stayed on Guam.

He shot one last order to Crusty, not caring how the hell the guy interpreted it. "I want Lurch assigned to watch Renshaw until she leaves."

Sprinting along the beach, Max whipped his T-shirt from his shoulders. His battered deck shoes pounded the mix of sand and ground coral.

He might not want to label the emotion that felt too close to an anticipation he hadn't experienced in two and half years. And he might not understand why it bothered him that Darcy Renshaw wanted a man who barely existed anymore.

But he knew without question he had to watch her every step, turn, move until he got her off the island.

She must have taken a wrong turn somewhere.

Darcy grasped a squat tangan-tangan tree for balance and wound her way down the moist dirt path. She kept the shore in sight as Max's assistant had told her. Meanwhile, the jungle seemed never ending.

Guam offered no half measures in bombarding the senses, and she found herself luxuriating in every step of the walk. Twining vines and flowers caressed her bare arms. Vibrant magentas and crimsons enthralled her eyes with their vibrancy, painted amidst emerald leaves of the tropical jungle. Wind drifted an intoxicating swell of hibiscus and philodendron perfumes.

A rush of hedonistic pleasure surged into sensory overload from a simple stroll. Not a response at all like her usual practical self. She couldn't help but wonder if the new awareness had something to do with a certain marine biologist with intriguing eyes and drop-dead awesome pecs.

Darcy cleared the palm trees into a thin patch of beach. A netted sea pen stretched across the lagoon. The gritty mix of coral and shells crunched beneath her tennis shoes. A dolphin arced through the glistening water below a low-slung coral ledge. Another finned back followed suit, but no trainer in sight.

Where was Max?

She scanned the beach, past the reef ledge over to the tree line. A flash of indigo and neon yellow snagged her attention with hues not found in any of the flowers she'd seen on the island.

Unless they were patterned on a pair of dive shorts.

Max jogged toward her while trees rustled with movement behind him.

A smile curved her lips. In a world full of military-issue drab olive, she found Max's unconventional flamboyance an intriguing change. That rebel quality called to her. A free spirit like him would understand her own need for soaring independence. With him, she could be herself, really fly. A guy like Max wouldn't smother her with overprotective urges.

With his every step, thick corded muscles rippled along his thighs. Damp hair matted his chest. Sunlight glinted an enticing call to her eyes straight down to his washboard abs.

Sprinting across the beach, Max tugged a raspberry-red T-shirt over his head. Which offered a perfect excuse to transfer her attention to his face.

His blue-green eyes met hers, eyes as sharp as any diamond edge. A shiver rippled through her, a tingling awareness that made her sensual walk through the jungle pale.

She'd made a grave tactical error.

This guy wasn't some ivory tower academic with minimal real-world experience. He wasn't even a simple beach bum with a brain.

Max Keagan was all man. Too much man. Especially for her.

Forget taking a stand. This might not be the wisest course of action. His eyes blazed with the experience of someone who'd lived more in thirty-some-odd years than most did in two lifetimes. Even if she had all the experience of Cleopatra and *Gunsmoke*'s Miss Kitty compacted into her own ordinary self, she should think twice about the wisdom of finishing her trek up the path.

Not that Max was going to leave her any options. He closed the distance between them, blocking her view of the jungle. "Well, Lieutenant, what brings you here?"

"Just wanted to check out your new dolphin digs." She edged back toward the trees. "But if it's not a convenient time, I can go." Not that she was in any great hurry to place that call to her father and have it out with him.

"No." His fingers wrapped around her arm to stop her. "Now's fine."

Max palmed the back of her waist and guided her in the opposite direction. She would have questioned his determination to redirect her steps, if she could have found words.

Thoughts fled. Sensations ruled. The heat of his splayed fingers steamed through her T-shirt. That piña colada scent saturated her senses, making her thirsty and so very hungry at the same time.

Her feet moved. Or at least they must have, since she found herself standing on a jagged coral ledge overlooking the lagoon. Max stopped beside her. His golden legs radiated heat that scorched the bare skin below her shorts.

From the corner of her eye, she studied him, her gaze lingering on the tattoo below his hacked-off sleeves. Nothing flashy or large. Just a simple diver-down symbol, a small red-and-white rectangle on his upper arm. Did tattooed skin feel different? Rougher, maybe? Her gaze traveled to the thin scar slicing beside it, disappearing into his shirt.

A hard man of so many textures.

His biceps rippled the pattern as he lifted his hand, put two fingers in his mouth and whistled. Three sharp blasts.

Darcy jolted. Almost pitched off the ledge. Just as she regained her balance, the water exploded in front of her. One dolphin, then another arced through the air, landing with a splash.

"Ohmigosh!"

A rusty chuckle slid from Max's throat as he palmed her waist again. "Easy, now, Lieutenant."

Beneath the clear water, the dolphins circled in perfect harmony until they stopped just shy of the ledge. Side by side, their heads popped above the water.

Max knelt. An elbow resting on his knee, he extended a hand. "Hi, there, girls." He glanced up at

Darcy. "I thought you'd like to meet them face-to-face."

She crouched beside him, unable to resist this peek into his world, a world so different from her own. "I understand intellectually how fast they are. But seeing all that power unleashed firsthand. Wow! It's just so..." She shrugged, picked at loose coral along the edge and flicked them into the water. "That probably sounds silly to you."

"Not at all. The day you lose respect for their strength is the day someone gets hurt."

Her gaze jerked to his face. Did he mean his words as a warning about himself, as well? One she should probably heed.

Each dolphin nudged his hand and received a stroke in turn. Those broad hands broadcast a similar restrained power. Magnetic strength.

Darcy pushed aside her fears as well as thoughts of taking a stand. Why not simply enjoy this moment with a man she found surprisingly as captivating as the prospect of a flight takeoff? "Which is which?"

He pointed left. "Lucy." Then right. "Ethel."

She stared at the pair of dolphins, both with gray-green backs fading into a white underbelly. "How do you tell them apart?"

"Every dolphin has a distinctive face and body markings. If you have a kennel full of beagles, they all look different. Or a pasture of horses. Or a room of people. Same with dolphins." A tree rustled behind them. Loose coral skittered down the cliff path. Max hooked a finger under her chin and guided her face toward the dolphins sticking their heads above water. "Look. Closer. Tell me what you see. Think details rather than the whole picture."

She narrowed her eyes until the two animals became more than just a bobbing duo, more than just twin "Flippers." "Lucy has a longer, uh—" Darcy gestured a circle around her mouth "—uh, snout?"

"Rostrum."

"Right. And Ethel has a bigger bump on her head. What's it called?"

"A melon."

"Melon? Really? Cool." So the ivory-tower dude lived within the dangerous hunk after all. How many layers were there to Max Keagan? "What are all those marks along the side?"

"Laminar flow lines. Friction marks from the water rushing along the rostrum and melon."

His words barely registered in her distracted brain. She stared into Max's eyes, eyes as changeable as the blue-green ripples of the ocean. In spite of all that water slapping the rock face, her mouth dried right up.

He turned away, thank heavens, before she made a fool out of herself. Again.

Max reached low and patted the rocks until Lucy moved closer. "Go ahead and pet her if you'd like."

Darcy stroked the bulbous melon, the rubbery skin damp and cool to the touch. A gray snout nudged her arm until she fell back on her bottom.

Laughing, she righted herself, sitting on her heels so as not to be caught unaware again. "Surprised me, didn't you, Lucy?" Darcy inched her hand forward, then hesitated to glance at Max. "What should I do differently?"

"Nothing. Keep on with what you're doing. Careful and steady." He reassured her as she rubbed the rostrum. "Watch for signs that they're agitated. Yes, they've been trained, but don't forget for a minute they're wild creatures first.''

Darcy's hand stopped midstroke. More warnings when dealing with the trainer as well as the dolphins? The man reminded her of that deceptively clear water luring her to jump in for a nice little swim, only to find currents and depths beyond what her limited experience would lead her to expect.

A careful woman might have backed off, and for five sane seconds earlier she'd considered it. Now she preferred to view her initial retreat as merely a wise tactical maneuver for regrouping.

Time to advance.

A Renshaw never backed down from a challenge, and this was her line-in-the-sand time. No more giving up what she wanted. And right now she wanted to kiss Max Keagan.

Max looked into Darcy's eyes and read her intent too damned well, easy enough to ID an echo of his own thoughts. Not smart at all, and he couldn't let her go for at least another five minutes until the intel contacts cleared the perimeter.

Ethel clicked and cackled a few feet away, bringing a return to reality with her demand for attention. Max couldn't decide whether to thank or curse his finned chaperone.

Darcy shifted, unfolding her legs and stretching out on her stomach along the rock. Her bare legs extended behind her in a mile-long, libido-assaulting display.

Reaching over the ledge, she wriggled her fingers. Again Lucy nudged Darcy. This time she kept her balance.

She smoothed a hand along Lucy's rostrum, even

allowing the dolphin to grip her hand inside her mouth and shake. Darcy's earlier hesitation had faded, replaced by a reckless abandon, an embrace-life attitude he recognized. A woman like that wouldn't be content with half measures from any relationship.

Relationship?

What the hell was he thinking? He'd known her all of three days. Within another couple of days, she would be winging her way back to the States and out of his life.

Max used the lull of the waterfall to restore his concentration. He needed to pace himself. The underwater search could take days, weeks even, before he located which offshore communications cable carried the tap. If at all.

At least Darcy would be gone by then. Max stretched out beside her as she placed her hand into Ethel's mouth for another shake. "You're very trusting."

"You wouldn't have let me touch them if you thought they would hurt me."

Her expression was so damned open he could fall right in.

Max set his jaw and studied the blood-red coral reef. He forced himself to think of another woman who'd believed in him. "Like I said. You're too trusting."

Pulling her hand from the dolphin's mouth, Darcy rolled to her side. Odd how she moved with more caution when approaching him than she had the wild beasts in the water.

Damned wise woman. Or maybe not.

She touched his arm. Lightly. Just one finger outlining the rectangular border of his tattoo. His skin burned beneath the soft pad of her finger with more heat than when the needle had marked him seventeen years ago in one of his countless moments of teenage rebellion.

What was it about this woman that turned near-innocent moves into a siren song?

Darcy continued the featherlight torment over the scar on his arm, tracing up into the edge of his sleeve. "What's life worth if we always play it safe?"

He grabbed her wrist. "That doesn't mean you should be reckless."

"Some risks are worth taking." Her eyes glinted with determination—and an underlying vulnerability that rocked him more than confronting armed divers guarding the drug runner's sub in South America.

Max knew what was coming long before her gaze dropped to his mouth. Knew he should stop her. Instead he held her wrist and stared back.

She kissed him, and heaven help him he didn't pull away.

Their eyes stayed open as he devoured her with his gaze, instead of an open mouth. A damned stupid thing to do, but how could he have known this simple act of trust from her would arouse him as much as if he'd kissed her the way his body begged him?

Darcy's mouth softened beneath his. Her pupils widened in a message of arousal that matched his own, just before her lashes fluttered close. Those generous lips of hers parted in an invitation he didn't stand a chance in hell of turning down.

The tide roared in his ears, giving him only a half second to realize a dolphin was approaching with a—

Splash.

Water sluiced over them in a lukewarm shower. Not nearly cold enough.

Darcy jerked back with a squeal. Max sat up, swiping the drops from his eyes.

Then regretted the move. Blurred vision proved much safer than a clear view of the goddess in a wet T-shirt sitting no less than twelve inches away. Soaked cotton molded to every curve and peak of her breasts, and man, had she ever hidden some generous curves beneath that flight suit.

Max cleared his throat, if not his thoughts, and hooked an elbow over his knee. "We shouldn't have done that."

"Why?" She trailed her fingers along his jaw in a gentle invitation. "I already want to do it again."

He scrambled for a face-saving out for her. "I'm not interested in starting something I don't stand a chance of finishing. We live on opposite coasts. I'll be here for weeks. You're going to leave in a couple of days."

Darcy's brow scrunched into that "I'm checking you out" frown, the one that made her bottom lip full and tempting. As if it needed any help. "What makes you think I'm leaving in two days?"

Uh-oh.

"Another day of cr—" He stopped himself cold before he slipped up and used the phrase "crew rest," military jargon a biology professor had no business knowing. Damn, but she had him too rattled. "Another day for your crew to rest up and then you're back to the States."

"Usually, yeah. But because of that earthquake in Taiwan, we're staying in Guam on stand-by to fly in relief supplies and bulldozers." Absently she plucked at her wet shirt, showcasing mermaid curves. "I'll be here for three weeks."

Foreboding mingled with an edgy thrill, and finally with a ragged fear. This was about more than turning away a woman who was wrong for him. About more than protecting her from tangling her life with a man who wanted nothing from a relationship except sex.

This was about keeping her well away from a situation that could turn deadly in a heartbeat.

Resisting Darcy for a couple of days was tough enough. Resisting those mermaid curves and siren eyes for three weeks straight would be damned near impossible.

And if he screwed up this mission, she could be the one to pay. A hell he vowed never to visit again.

Chapter 4

Robin flicked a spider off the crumbling World War II–era bunker and took a front row seat on the cement box for the lovelorn scenario unfolding on the beach below with Max and his lady pilot. No need to hide in the brush. Lurking would only look suspicious.

I have as much right to watch the sunset as they do.

Robin traced the slits along the camouflaged bunker, stroking the tiny openings for guns in battle like a talisman. Robin inched closer. Sure Max would be irritated if he saw his audience of one, since he'd demanded the beach stay clear. But he'd just have to get over it. Keeping track of Max's every move was essential.

Boring. But essential.

The jungle edged right up to the shoreline. Historic invasions had occurred here, the perfect site for a modern-day battle if only Max would look up and wonder. Just a hundred or so yards separated them, not far at all if Max were focusing on anything other than the woman with him. Interesting.

Max cupped her shoulders. Then carefully set her away. Renshaw moved forward, but Max kept her firmly at arm's distance.

Apparently make-out time was over.

Too bad the crashing waterfall muffled their conversation, but even without the words, it became increasingly clear Max was giving her the brush-off. Not surprising since he hadn't shown more than a short-term interest in any woman since Eva.

Eva.

The need to hurt Max, badly, surged to the surface. Robin tucked the beach bag closer. The hefty 9mm inside rasped along the rough cement surface, taunting with how easy it would be to tuck inside the bunker, make use of those gun slits and end it all, warrior-style.

Wasn't two and a half years long enough to wait?

But to act prematurely would toss away meticulously plotted revenge. Years of subtle torture. Watching Max shred himself up with guilt had been downright entertaining.

Silhouetted by the sunset, Max stood, clasping Darcy's hand to pull her to her feet.

Robin saw the very moment Max realized they weren't alone. The slight narrowing of his eyes, followed by a quick scan of the perimeter.

Beating yourself up over losing focus and missing me here, are you? Good. Robin savored the victory and called out, "Well, hello there."

Max nodded.

Darcy dropped Max's hand. "Hi. I didn't see you walking up. Uh...been here long?"

"For a while. Mind if I join you?" Robin side-stepped stones down the rocky path to the coral out-cropping, clutching the bag of sunscreen, binoculars, night vision goggles and a 9mm. "I've heard this is the best spot on the island for taking in the sunset."

Swiping an arm over his forehead, Max dried away beads of sea spray mingling with sweat. "Another time. The spot's all yours." He urged Darcy forward. "Let's get moving back to the base before those clouds open up."

"Bye." She tossed a quick smile over her shoulder. "Enjoy the sunset."

"I plan to." Robin smiled back, all the while think-ing how this woman's rough-and-tumble style paled next to Eva's exotic elegance.

Max palmed Darcy's waist, ushering her around the tree and up the hill. Robin eyed their backs, a hand gravitating down to caress the concealed weapon.

The couple faded from sight, but Max's profile im-age as they'd left stayed imprinted in Robin's mem-ory. A one-second, unguarded look from the man and Robin knew. The guy wasn't as immune to Darcy Renshaw as he wanted her to believe.

Maybe the ever-honorable Max had pushed her away because of his undercover mission. Or maybe out of lingering feelings for Eva.

Not that the reasons mattered in the least.

Absently smacking at a bug crawling into the bag, Robin continued to stare after them, a diversionary plan creeping to completion. The wait wouldn't have to be so boring after all.

Unnerving one little "wren" would be far more

effective than a direct threat to Max. Upset Renshaw to upset Max. Thanks to insider intel on background checks for all parties involved, Robin knew just how to start.

Luckily, plenty of pests for unsettling an airborne wren scurried right on the ground.

Darcy charged up the carved-out dirt steps as fast as her tennis shoes would carry her. Her brain refused to focus on anything more than returning to her room in the VOQ, Visiting Officer's Quarters.

One little kiss and she was a mess.

Okay, so it wasn't exactly a *little* kiss. It had been more like a double-time scramble takeoff, from dead stop to airborne in less than five minutes.

She'd expected to enjoy it—a lot. She hadn't expected to have her mind flipped, as if that incredible takeoff had gone rogue in a heartbeat, inverting into tailspin. Even now, she couldn't tell up from down as she stumbled along the path toward the vine-covered Spanish bridge arching over a stream.

And more than anything, Darcy did not like being out of control.

Max's steady steps and breaths kept pace behind her. The heat of his chest radiated a constant reminder of the fire of his response. Her experience might fall short of her sister's, but it didn't take a rocket scientist to conclude Max had been attracted, too. Impressively so.

Not that he seemed particularly happy about it. The ill-disguised horror in his eyes when he'd heard she would be staying for three weeks relayed an oceanful of his real feelings on the subject of taking that kiss any further.

How flippin' humiliating. What had she been think-ing? She'd thrown herself at the guy like some sex-starved maniac. Now that her frustration and anger at her father had cooled to a simmer, she viewed her blatant come-on to a man she barely knew with some-thing akin to self-disgust. And that there had been a witness to her humiliation standing a few yards away…

Ugh!

Darcy plucked at her clammy shirt, still damp from the dolphins' dousing. She just wanted to make it back to her room with her dignity in tact. Soak in a hot shower. And slowly die of mortification.

Her rental car waited just beyond the lush line of trees. Time was running out if she wanted to close the book on the mess she'd made without more witnesses.

Darcy turned to walk backward. "About the drink thing. We should probably just skip it."

Max cocked his head to the side, studying her like some mysterious new organism under his microscope. "If that's what you want."

Hello!

Of course it wasn't what she wanted, but she'd al-ready ruined any chance for easing into something simple. The real kicker was that she'd enjoyed talking to him, and now she'd blown even that. Nothing left to do but save face and cut him loose before she em-barrassed herself further.

Or weakened and hit on him again. "You were right about not starting anything since we live on dif-ferent coasts."

Max watched water bead from Darcy's slicked hair, down her neck and into her T-shirt. What he wouldn't give to dive right into that drop of water.

Damn, but he had to get his head on straight and quit thinking with his libido. If this woman had that much power over him with one near-innocent kiss, diving completely into that whirlpool of heat would level him.

The hell of it was that while he should keep his distance, he also wanted to keep tabs on her until she left. Like dribbling water on a parched man's tongue.

Another drop beaded from her hair, down her brow, falling, catching and holding on her lips.

Better not think about water. "Sure. And it's not like either of us has a flexible work schedule while we're here."

"Absolutely, and back home I'm TDY all over the world two-thirds of the year," she answered, jumping all over the line of excuses.

Too bad he still wanted to jump all over her. "I'm always in class, in the lab or on the road."

"Real workaholic." She backed along the dirt path.

"So I've been told." He picked up her lead, following with his words as well as his steps.

"Hey, that's how it is when you love your job."

"Uh-huh." He reached to swipe a drooping branch out of her way. The lean brought him too close. A couple inches farther and he would taste Darcy and the lingering salt of the sea and her sunflower seeds.

"This is a critical time for you."

"Right."

"You don't need distractions."

"You said it." With those legs wrapped around his waist, he would definitely be distracted.

"And neither do I."

"I don't even like sunflower seeds." *Liar.* He liked the taste just fine on her lips.

"Well then." Her grin lit her face as well as her eyes. "You're history, pal."

Her feet danced back inches from stepping off the path into a tangle of vines.

"Watch out!" Max grabbed her shoulders, soft shoulders in spite of all the toned muscle flexing beneath his touch. His thumbs stroked of their own volition.

They both stood, the plush ground giving beneath their feet like a feather bed. Her pupils widened. The humidity in the air upped, at least it must have since every breath felt thicker. Their newfound ease evaporated in a snap.

Damn.

A great big distraction and her legs weren't anywhere near his waist.

Darcy licked the drop from her lips. "I need to go."

Bugs hummed in the trees as neither of them moved. A foot-long lizard scuttled past.

She opened her mouth again as if to say something else, then shook her head, shrugging from under his hands. "Goodbye, Max."

"Good night," he answered to her retreating back, wondering why he couldn't let her just keep walking right on out of his life. She wasn't his responsibility, especially not since he'd just assigned Lurch to tail her. Besides, she could protect herself with the training she'd received, compliments of Uncle Sam. Darcy Renshaw did *not* need Max's protection.

Darcy jogged up the path, her flexing calves offering a too-enticing view. He allowed himself the pleasure of watching until she slipped around a thatch of trees and out of sight.

She might not need him, but that wouldn't stop him

from checking. Max swacked a branch aside and headed back for the beach. Darcy couldn't run far enough for his peace of mind on a water-locked island where too many vermin scuttled under every rock.

Reaching into her flight bag, Darcy searched by touch for her lunch during their final approach to Guam. The past week of hauling everything from bulldozers to food rations into Taiwan had left her with little time for sleeping. Forget about regular meals.

Worse yet, today's mission off-loading medical supplies had been too turbulence-ridden for her to scarf down even a sandwich. She planned to make the most of the ten minutes before transition, touch-and-go landings.

Darcy fished out an apple and polished it on the leg of her flight suit. Max had been right. They were both too busy to breathe, much less indulge in a wild, fantasy-worthy fling on a sandy beach.

If only she didn't feel his eyes on her every time she turned around.

Yanking her mind back to work, Darcy finished punching in the landing coordinate data into the C-17's computerized instrument panel. Her job was too important to her to risk it for anyone, no matter how hot or interesting. She lived to fly. She thrived on making a difference, and while today's mission might not have been Cantou-kick-butt material, she'd made her mark. She didn't know any other way of life.

Darcy pressed the interphone button to check in with the aircraft commander in the left seat. "Landing calculations complete," she reported, crunching a bite of her apple.

The plane bucked. She grabbed for her green military bag as it slid toward the floor. "Hey, Crusty, how about give me heads-up next time you opt for acrobatics."

"No problem," Daniel Baker slid a finger under the earpiece of his headset. "If you'll warn me before you blow out my eardrum crunching your lunch. Or better yet, let's go to hot mike so I can hear every bite."

Laughing, Darcy pitched a wadded napkin at him. "Bite this, *sir.*"

"They sure breed copilots mouthy these days."

"I try my best." Darcy flipped the microphone to the side while she finished her apple.

The plane flying wingman eased into view, high and to the right. Bronco manned the helm, flashing a thumbs-up just before the headset crackled with his voice. "Way to pound through the skies. Did Crusty just take over the controls?"

Baker snorted. "Funny."

"What kind of flying they call that?"

"Good," Baker quipped without hesitation. "We're talking real, warrior flying, in case you didn't recognize it when you saw it. The kind that makes lesser men hurl."

"Well, go easy on your wren. Wouldn't want her ralphing up her lunch."

Darcy thumbed the mike button. "Not a chance of that."

Laughter filtered over the headset as the other plane held steady, one of the C-17s from McChord AFB. The Washington squadron had deployed a detachment unit to assist with the relief effort, packing Guam with cargo crewmen. Today Bronco crewed with his old

buddy Major Grayson "Cutter" Clark, a dual qualified pilot and flight surgeon.

Crusty tore the wrapper off a Snickers bar with his
teeth as he flew. "Guam approach, Reach one-four-
five-two, lead aircraft level at twenty-one thousand
feet, wingman level at twenty-two thousand. Request
one turn around the island before landing."

"Roger, Reach one-four-five-three," the control
tower acknowledged. "You are the only traffic in my
scope. Cleared for one turn around the island. Call me
when ready for landing instructions."

Darcy pitched aside her apple core just as they descended to seven hundred feet for a low-level approach to the island. She enjoyed this part of her job,
seeing the world at its best from a primo box seat.
Bird's-eye views didn't come any more magnificent
than this. Waves crashed in foaming white breakers
against the shoreline of the dormant volcano land
base.

Crusty was a blast to crew with, fun and edgy in
the air, likely a holdover from his test-pilot days. He
knew just how far to push performance boundaries for
his craft. Like a kid gripping a joystick, he guided the
C-17 in a soaring low-level approach that rippled the
surf. Transparent water revealed the wreckage of a
Japanese freighter below.

Crusty circled around a cove, a speedboat easing
into sight. "Well, lookie there." The boat bobbed as
a diver hauled himself up the back ladder. Sun glinted
off the water as the diver combed his hand through
his spiky hair.

"Three guesses as to who that is." Crusty shot
Darcy a piercing, curious look. "Hey, you remember
the dolphin dude, don't you?"

"Uh-huh." Tough to forget about a guy when she bumped into him every time she turned around. Who'd have thought the island was so flippin' small? Everywhere she went, she felt like someone was three steps behind her.

Crusty waggled the wings in greeting. Max stretched a hand in greeting, bringing his other hand to his mouth. To whistle?

A dolphin exploded from the water, arcing over the bow of the boat, followed quickly by the second. Regret whispered through her over things not meant to be. Worse yet, she'd made things awkward between them so she couldn't even enjoy talking to him about his work.

"Hey, Wren," Crusty said over the headset as he angled into the turn to circle the island. "Do you have anything in there besides apples? Preferably something with lethal fat content."

Darcy pulled her gaze off Max and back to her job. "How about a PBJ?"

"Not chocolate, but it'll do in a pinch."

Why couldn't she have been attracted to Captain Snickers Bar instead? His rumpled good looks garnered a steady supply of women wanting to "fix" him. Smooth his disheveled, coffee-brown hair. Iron his rumpled flight suit. Bring him meals so he didn't die from junk food overload.

Crusty jammed the last half of the candy bar in his mouth. He definitely made a better fling candidate. Except for a few minor problems: she didn't date military men; she wasn't attracted to Crusty.

And she still wanted Max.

Darcy opened her fight bag and pitched aside her checklist. Digging deeper, she shoved through charts, an orange, the gun she'd been issued prior to the first flight to Taiwan because of looting riots after the earthquake. Finally she found the half-mashed peanut butter and jelly sandwich.

Pain stabbed her hand. Up her arm.

"Ouch!" She whipped her hand out. A spider scurried across her wrist. A big, ugly spider the size of a small dog—or a half-dollar—latched on. Darcy flicked her hand.

"Holy crap!" Crusty shouted. "What's that?"

She didn't want to think about what it was. She just wanted it the hell off her.

Now.

Darcy grabbed her checklist. A quick swipe sent the spider to the floor. The hairy eight-legged spawn of Satan scuttled toward the rudders.

Toward her feet.

The last thing she needed was that minimonster climbing up her leg during landing. Darcy stomped. Hard. Ground the toe of her boot until spider guts oozed.

Gross, but vengefully reassuring.

"Wow, Wren. If this Air Force gig doesn't work out for you, maybe you should consider a career as an exterminator."

"Probably pays better." Darcy forced the light-hearted answer.

"You okay?"

She examined the bite. Two tiny puncture marks. Red but not swollen, they seemed benign enough. "Positively zippy."

Darcy eased her boot off the spider.

She hated bugs. Truly hated them with a passion born of smothering fear. Not that she would ever admit such a wimpy feminine weakness to the rest of the aircrew. Survival training after flight school had been hellish with all the creepy-crawlies, but at least she'd steeled herself to expect them. Being caught unaware, however, sucked.

The headset crackled again. "Well, Crusty," Bronco called, "who do you have flying now, the loadmaster?"

Darcy depressed the interphone button. "Just a little upset in the cockpit thanks to a surprise stowaway."

"*Little,* my aunt Emmy Sue!" Crusty barked. "A nasty ol' Guam spider crawled out of Renshaw's bag and bit her."

"Spider?" Cutter interrupted from the other plane, his serious doctor tones overriding more easygoing pilot tones. "What kind?"

"A dead one." Darcy eyed the glob of spider pâté by her boot. The latest of many she'd stomped in the past week. There'd obviously been some kind of insect infestation since she'd been here last, either that or she'd become a bug magnet.

"Damn it," Cutter clipped through the headset. "Quit playing around and describe the thing to me."

Fear tingled up her spine like an encore spider bite. Most of the bugs on the island weren't poisonous. Right?

Darcy whipped off her glove and swept up her cuff to examine the two puncture wounds more closely. "I was too busy shaking the thing off to do a scientific classification, but I guess it was about the size of a fifty-cent piece. Hairy. Kind of colorful, green and brown. A red stripe maybe."

Cutter's sigh drifted over the headset. "Okay, no sweat, that sounds like an Orb-Web spider."

"Which is good?"

"Yeah. Mean-looking fella with long fangs for a big-time bite, but harmless otherwise," he clipped through the prognosis. "Just to be on the safe side, though, let's scratch the touch-and-gos and do a full stop so I can take a look at that bite."

Relief soothed the sting to her nerves as well as her skin.

"Sure, whatever you think's best, Doc." Darcy kept her voice steady, sinking back in her seat while Crusty and Bronco called in the adjusted landing schedule to the flight tower.

Darcy willed away the residual hum of nerves. The spider was dead, and she wasn't a kid in a prison cell being taunted by her captors. Bugs and snakes may have immobilized her into silence then, but she wasn't thirteen anymore.

She forced herself to drag her boot over the dead spider again. No, she wasn't a child anymore. But she'd sure as hell been acting like some adolescent around Max Keagan. Time to take responsibility for her actions and clear the air.

Darcy staunchly shushed the little voice telling her she was only making excuses of another kind to see him because she was rattled and needed a distraction.

She stared out the windscreen, watching Max guide the boat along the shoreline. Talking to him would be the wise and mature thing to do. She might be drop-dead tired, but she had a feeling sleep wouldn't be peaceful tonight anyhow.

Once Cutter gave her the medical all-clear, she definitely saw a swim and an apology in her future.

Chapter 5

So much for the day's swim. Max steered the boat away from the dolphin pen, toward the secluded cove where he docked his boat. A school of fish streaked alongside in a rainbow stream of color. He'd already penned the restless dolphins early at the University of Guam facilities due to the incoming storm. Fruitless searches frustrated the animals as much as their trainer.

He reminded himself that eliminating locales could be considered progress. He'd accepted early on the search could take weeks. Yet somewhere between the briefing room in San Diego and the airstrip in Guam the wait had become unacceptable. He wanted to clear this case and clear his mind of a certain tempting lady pilot. Soon.

No matter how many times he told himself Darcy Renshaw wasn't his problem, he couldn't stop keeping tabs on her the past week. He didn't have a concrete reason for the niggling apprehension. Probably had more to do with testosterone than any threat.

Except he'd lived undercover too long to ignore the value of following his instincts. Even if Lurch hadn't reported anything suspicious, Max's instincts told him to watch out for Darcy until she got the hell off the island. Damn it, there was a traitor on the inside, all the more reason to rely on no one.

Max rounded a coral reef into the secluded cove where he moored his boat. A cove that should have been deserted. Except his own mermaid siren waited to lure him in.

Lounging on a sandbar a few yards from shore, Darcy sat with her chin on her knees, soaking up the muted sun as storm clouds billowed overhead. Miles of leg stretched from her one-piece black swimsuit. Not one of those decorative scraps of Lycra, but a suit designed more for practicality than enticement. Somehow the subtler invitation tempted him all the more.

And of course there were those dog tags nestled between her breasts.

Max cut the engine power and coasted toward the dock. He tied the boat off, all the while conscious of her eyes on his every move.

Darcy cupped a hand to her mouth. "Ten bucks says you can't name all the kids from the *Brady Bunch*, in order."

After a too-damned long, frustrating day, he didn't have the energy or will to resist her. Max pitched the anchor overboard. "Actors or their television character names?"

"Characters."

"Too easy." He jumped into the shallow surf and waded toward her, waves lapping his waist. "I wouldn't feel right taking the hard-earned money of a government employee.''

''You're too nice.''

''Hardly.'' He closed in on her, stepping up onto the sandbar. ''I thought you were flying today.''

''We landed early.''

Early? Max dropped to sit beside her, instincts itching overtime like the sand coating his legs. ''Nothing wrong with the mission, I hope.''

''Nope. Picture perfect.'' Her arm draped over her knees, she drew circles in the sand with exaggerated concentration. ''We landed and off-loaded supplies in twenty minutes. Never even shut down engines before it was time to clear the ramp for the next formation of planes.''

With bitten fingernails that made him wonder and even worry, she continued to sketch in the sand until her canvas of circles expanded as wide as her silence.

Something wasn't right. Like her missing smile. The edginess in a normally indomitable woman. What was she doing here? ''So you decided to sunbathe.''

Darcy snorted inelegantly. ''I'm not exactly the sun goddess type. I just like to swim. When Dad was a squadron commander here in Guam, my sister, brother and I all but lived in the water. Snorkeling. Scuba. We loved to explore the underwater wreckages of the planes and boats.''

Where was she going with this? He might not know, but he would hang on for the ride long enough to wipe away whatever had brought the pucker of worry between her brows. ''Being stationed in Charleston near the beach works well for you then.''

''I fly a lot. That limits how often I can dive with the twenty-four-hour restriction before and after a flight because of the whole issue of nitrogen in the bloodstream.''

Max nodded. The extreme changes in pressure caused nitrogen bubbles to gather in the bloodstream. It only took one nitrogen bubble to the heart for things to turn deadly.

There was a lesson in that, no doubt. Their very different worlds of air and water weren't meant to coexist any more than he and Darcy.

Darcy abandoned her sand doodles. ''You've probably guessed I didn't just happen to be here coincidentally today.''

''Why are you here?'' He readied himself for anything from a woman who had an uncanny knack for leveling him.

''I want to apologize.''

Well, hell. A knockout before the first round. And what a knockout she was without even trying. ''Apologize for what?''

''For making things awkward.'' She drew her knees in tight, the wind whipping her cinnamon-brown hair around her face as she rested her chin on her folded hands. The storm brewing in the skies echoed the one in her eyes.

''There's nothing to apol—''

''Please, stop. This is embarrassing enough, but I need to say it.'' The red burning her cheeks had nothing to do with the sun. ''I'm not good at this kind of thing. I'm even worse at talking about it.''

Max prayed she'd get the hell off the subject of kissing, fast, which led too easily to thoughts of laying Darcy back on that sandbar and investigating her tan lines.

She straightened, her arms falling away from her

knees as she braced her shoulders for battle. "Okay, here goes. I made a real pest out of myself back on the beach the other day and you were nice to let me off the hook with all those bicoastal excuses. You're a sexy, fascinating guy, but I realize you're not interested. And that's fine." She paused, laughing lightly as she scrunched her toes in the sand. "Well, sort of."

Her honesty was killing him faster than bullets.

Waves rolled up the sandbar, lapping around them before receding. "I'm not any good at games, Max, and I just misread the signs. Sorry. Most of all, I'm sorry I've made things uncomfortable this past week."

He felt slimier than pond scum. How did he combat such total, open honesty? Especially when she had every reason to be pissed at him. He'd sent mixed signals from the start. Here was his chance to fix that by sending her safely packing. Cut her off. Now.

He couldn't do it. He had to offer her some kind of a face-saving out while still keeping the boundaries in place. "You didn't misread anything."

Confusion creased her brow—with an unmistakable hope glinting in her eyes.

Rule number two for undercover work, keep the story as close to the truth as possible. He forced the words out. "There's someone else."

Her brow smoothed.

But the wary hope faded also. "Oh, well, that explains it then. I should have thought to ask at the start."

"Or rather there *was.*" Where had that come from? Hell. Her honesty must be an infectious disease.

Darcy rested her cheek on her knees and watched him, waiting without pushing. This woman made talking easy.

Too easy.

"She, uh…" Max looked away from those amber-rich eyes luring him to spill secrets. He scooped up a shell, pitching it from hand to hand. "She died two and a half years ago."

"I'm so sorry."

The soft comfort of her words washed over him like the incoming tide. Not effusive or gushing. But genuine.

He regulated his breathing with the steady rhythm of toss, catch, toss, catch. "We'd been living together for about six months, had even started to talk about getting married."

Max shoved thoughts of the baby aside. He didn't want to open himself up to that much honesty today. Or ever. He pitched the shell into the ocean that had taken Eva as well as their kid away from him.

"How horribly unfair."

"Yeah, it was." He'd been the one who should have died. Survivor's guilt was hell to live with.

The normal constraints he kept on his emotions slipped. He'd channeled it all into revenge for so long, he didn't know what to do with the churn threatening to kick over him.

Why couldn't he just sleep with Darcy since they both wanted it? He could lose himself inside her for a few hours. He'd done so more than a few times over the past two and a half years. Except the women he'd chosen had been using him as much as he'd been using them. That wouldn't be the case with Darcy, and then he would have even more guilt heaped on top of an already weighty load.

Yeah, he wanted her all the way down to his waterlogged toes, but he wouldn't do anything about it.

"You're an..." He paused, brushing a thumb over a raindrop on her cheek and thanked God it wasn't a tear. He searched for the words to do her justice, but had to settle for, "an incredibly hot lady. But I'm not in a good place right now and the last thing I need is to drag someone down there with me." Understatement of the year.

"Incredibly hot?" She gently slugged his arm. "Well, Doc, you sure do know how to make a girl feel good when you're letting her down."

He wanted to tell her to shower her compassion on somebody else. He didn't need it or deserve it. He'd only told her the bit about Eva for calculated reasons, not out of any honest intent to share something from his past. Every inch of him wanted to shout at her to stop trusting him.

Raindrops picked up speed, pocking the water and offering a convenient excuse to run from a conversation that was shifting into dangerous territory. "We should head in before the clouds open up. Come on and I'll walk you to your quarters."

The words backfired in his brain as he faced another night of not sleeping while thinking of her two doors down. Just his luck, the Air Force had been accommodating in providing him and his assistant with VOQ rooms under the guise of accommodating the whole "free the dolphins" mission. Sure being on base offered additional security, but at a lethal price to his sanity.

Max stood, stomping sand off and extending his hand to Darcy without thinking. Until her fingers twined with his. Then he couldn't think of anything except the way she felt.

Max flipped her hand in his. An excuse to touch

her a while longer? Maybe. A small white bandage glinted on her wrist, puckered from water but holding strong. "What happened here?"

"Spider bite. No big deal."

She shuddered, only a small tremble so imperceptible he wouldn't have known if he hadn't been holding her hand.

"There are plenty of those around here. Don't forget to shake your boots out before putting them on."

"I'm used to the buggers showing up in my room." A light laugh slipped free at odds with the tiny tremor. "But the ugly thing stowed away in my flight bag behind my lunch. Actually, that's why we landed early. Doc Clark wanted to make sure it wasn't poisonous."

Poisonous. The word twisted something inside Max, and he didn't like it. Damn it, it was just a freaking spider bite. The woman was a combat-ready military officer. She didn't need his misplaced overprotective urges.

He forced his thumb to still. Max dropped her hand, clearing his throat and thoughts as he stepped back. "I'm glad you're all right."

Thunder rumbled a warning just before the skies opened up in a tropical downpour. Darcy slicked back her hair, a full-out wicked smile on her lips. "Last one to the VOQ's a sea turtle. Ready. Set."

She shoved him backward into the surf and sprinted away.

"Go!" she shouted over her shoulder already halfway to shore as she splashed through the surf. Her laughs carried along the wind, whipping round him. Open, playful, free of concerns and full of life.

He intended to make sure that didn't change.

* * *

Screams swelled in Darcy's throat.

She jammed her face into the pillow to stifle the shout begging to burst free. The half-awake side of her brain struggled to smother nightmare cries with reason.

Spiders only crawled in her dreams now.

Snakes only slithered through her subconscious.

Still the coiling pressure around her leg seemed so real. Tighter and tighter it gripped, painful even through her sleep-dazed senses. Darcy flipped to her back. Listened to rain pattering outside. Worked to will away the fog of sleep.

"Okay. Wake up." She scissored her legs free from the tangled sheets. Her left leg felt sluggish. Perhaps numbed asleep. Something like exercise weights strapped to her ankle anchored it to the bed.

Cold, scaly weights.

Oh, God.

This wasn't a dream.

Darcy snapped awake and upright just as fangs sank into her skin. Hot pain flashed up her calf. Terror spiked through her harder than whatever had hold of her leg.

Only seconds earlier, screams had seemed impossible to restrain. Now she couldn't push a single squawk past a constriction in her throat tighter than the grip on her leg.

She blinked against the pitch-black darkness. Why had she chosen tonight of all nights to roll down the hurricane shutters? She grappled for the lamp.

The needle-like fangs sank deeper. Pressure increased. It couldn't be as heavy as it felt. Surely fear exaggerated sensations. If only she'd worn sweats to sleep tonight rather than the cooler ribbed T-shirt and panties.

Her clammy fingers fumbled with the switch. The lamp wobbled, tipped, clattered to the floor. Her first muffled whimpers of fear whispered free.

Please, someone hear me. Help me.

Echoes of childhood whimpers for rescue, quiet pleadings she'd prayed someone would hear on a psychic level because she wasn't allowed to scream or they would bring back the spiders. Or the snakes.

Just small, green garden snakes, she reminded herself. Her kidnappers hadn't wanted to risk damaging their collateral.

The thick coil began to unfurl along her leg, jaws still clamped on to her.

Her pulse pounded in her ears like the rap-rap-rap of helicopter blades beating the air. What if the snake released her ankle? She swallowed back bile at thoughts of it biting her stomach.

Her face.

The pressure eased. A slow serpentine glide started up the outside of her leg. Panic clawed at her insides.

She forced herself to think. It wasn't moving quickly. She just needed light to dial the phone for help. Quietly. If she stayed calm, someone could get the key and come for help.

Someone?

Her mind blanked of all room numbers except Max's. Of course he was the logical choice. The man worked with animals. Max would know what to do.

Carefully, she inched her hand across the coverlet. She stifled the urge to flail against the insidious caress inching toward her hip.

Her fingertips brushed the light. Steady this time.

Max might even have the perfect answer for her over the phone. Once she gave him a description of the snake, he would reassure her it wasn't poisonous. Then she would just hang out with her fanged buddy until her own personal exterminator found a key.

Darcy twisted the switch. Harsh yellow light sent sparks pricking in front of her until her eyes adjusted. She blinked, focused and turned to face her attacker.

Beady eyes the size of dimes stared back from the foot of her bed.

Full-blown nausea born of terror roiled. Her dreams hadn't been an exaggeration at all. Obsidian eyes seared her from the head of a ten-foot-long brown snake as big around as her white-knuckled fist.

Max! she mentally screamed without twitching even a muscle. Her gaze jerked back to the bedside table. No phone waited beneath the light.

Frantically she traced the path of the telephone cord across the room. Fifteen feet away. It might as well have been miles. The phone rested beneath the window where she'd left it when she'd called her sister before going to bed.

Darcy drew in a shaky breath, using every ounce of training to squash her terror. Help wasn't within reach, and damn it, she'd learned to deal with pests in survival. Which left her with only one option.

Time to kick some snake butt herself. She just hoped the reptile wasn't looking for supper.

Unwrapping his turkey-sandwich supper, Max settled behind the laptop computer resting on the utilitarian table in his VOQ room. He clicked through the multiple menus, logging into the remote account linking him to the CIA's mainframe computer.

Rain gurgled through the gutters outside his door while he waited for the connection to complete. He bit off half the sandwich. Scratched a hand over his bare chest. And tried not to think how much better his day could have ended if he'd been two doors down in the room with Darcy.

The secured black-and-green screen hummed to life, snagging his attention back to the job at hand: sending his report. The list of additional captioned addresses stretched like a damned laundry list. Why worry about a tap leaking military plans when he was all but using a freaking bullhorn transmitting his reports to a stadium?

Not much of a team player are you, son? his father's voice taunted through the years.

Sure he was. He'd just found his animals respected rules and loyalty better. Max tipped back in his chair to open the small fridge behind him for a bottle of water.

A pop cut the air.

A gunshot.

His chair slammed back onto all fours. He shut down thought. Training assumed control. Max nailed the terminate button on his computer with one hand as he grabbed for his Glock with the other.

A second shot rattled the windows.

Close.

Adrenaline pumped through him. He didn't question his instincts. He knew.

Two rooms down. Darcy.

He tore out the door and into the night air as a third shot reverberated. He blasted down the walkway past Lurch, already sprinting in the same direction. Doors flung open above them, feet pounding, heads peering over the balcony.

Max reached the door first. He twisted the knob. Locked. "Damn it." He shouldered the door. Not that it budged. "Darcy, talk to me."

Silence.

Lurch crowded behind him. "You wanna kick it in or should I?"

"Move. I've got it." Max backed a step. Gun up and ready, he kicked the door once, twice.

The panel crashed inward. Leading with his Glock, Max swung into the gaping doorway.

And confronted the very last scenario he would have expected. Hell, he couldn't have ever envisioned this one.

Darcy lay on her side on the floor beside the bed, legs tangled around bed sheets and...a snake.

Relief warred with a new dread.

Her arms extended and taut, she aimed her gun at the ten-foot twitching serpent. A snake whose head wasn't more than six inches away from her. With a striking distance half of its length, the creature would have a reach far beyond what it would take to nail Darcy.

A brown tree snake—he identified quickly—it only carried mild venom. Not a problem. Unless it struck repeatedly.

Max eased into the room. Closer. Careful to keep his movements unthreatening, he extended his hand, ready to immobilize the undoubtedly pissed reptile. "Darcy, you can stop. I'll take care of him."

Her hand clenched around the trigger.

"Easy now." Max held still, kept his voice even, hoping to calm the woman as much as the snake.

''Shift that gun to the side. I can stop this fella faster and safer than any more bullets. Okay?''

Her finger slid off the trigger. Her throat moved with a long swallow.

Slowly, he placed the gun on the floor. No sudden moves until…he…was…

Ready.

His hand shot forward. His fingers locked around the snake. Just behind its powerful jaws. Immobilizing its mouth.

Relief, too much, churned through him. He shoved it aside before it distracted him.

Max didn't have to debate what to do next. Given the need to control the tree snake population on Guam, the fact that it was near death anyhow and that the damned thing had scared the tough-as-nails Darcy pale, the snake would die. A quick snap and he put the snake out of its misery.

Max hefted aside the limp reptile and crouched by Darcy. ''You okay?''

She elbowed up, wincing. ''Positively zippy.''

And nearly naked.

Now that the initial crisis had faded, his eyes took in Darcy sprawled on her side. And there was plenty of her to see.

Sweet mercy and The Doors, the woman was so hot she could make a man forget how to swim. ''Take a second to catch your breath.''

While he found his.

Her matching panties and ribbed tank top, some kind of pale-orange color with flowers patterned over every enticing inch, weren't the garb he found on most sharpshooters. But the dichotomy added a sexy edge to Darcy's vibrancy. Sure he'd scoped out her legs earlier, but the whole bedroom setup with her breasts full and unrestrained against the ribbed shirt sent his every molecule of testosterone to full chemical boil.

Not that he imagined she would want the growing crowd, or even him, checking her out right now.

Max nudged his gun under the bed and out of sight as he reached over her shoulder to drag the spread off the mattress. His bare chest brushed her damned near bare one. No lingering there, chump. Especially not with the group of gawkers standing behind them and Darcy's pupils still dilated with fear.

Adrenaline and anger pulsed overtime even as he told himself she would be fine. One cranky brown snake wouldn't bring down this woman who didn't have a wilting-flower cell in her body.

He wrapped the blanket around her, tucking her orange underwear out of sight. "Here you go."

Later he would think about why the hell it was so important to shield her from everyone's eyes but his own.

"Thanks, Max." Darcy's grip whitened on the blanket, her breaths ragged but her voice steady. "For the blanket and for taking care of Sly over there."

"My part was small." He clenched his hands to stop from stroking her back, offering some kind of comfort. "You were holding your own just fine."

"Whatever."

From the parking lot, a shout for people to get the hell out of the way sounded just before Crusty shoved into the room. He screeched to a halt by the snake.

"Holy crap." Shoving a hand through a major case of bed head, Daniel Baker whistled long and slow. "Remind me to request you as my wingman next time I'm flying combat."

She laughed, her voice thin and too tight. "Maybe I'll let *you* be *my* wingman, Baker."

"Dream on." He scratched a hand along the shoulder of his inside-out shirt. "Are you okay, co?"

"She's fine now." Max's hand curved around her shoulder. Crusty's gaze fell right down to Max's possessive grip. Yeah, he was staking sunflower-seed rights. If he was wrong for Darcy, then the dark-ops tester dude in front of him wasn't any better for her.

Darcy angled to peek around Max. "Anybody see Doc Clark out there in the hall? I've got a little problem."

Her lighthearted grin betrayed by her chalky face, she swept aside the corner of the spread to reveal three sets of puncture wounds climbing up her ankle to her knee.

She adjusted her hold on the blanket, the Band-Aid from her spider bite earlier setting off alarms in Max's head.

Two accidental attacks in one day.

Suspicion coiled into certainty in Max's gut. He'd learned fast not to believe in coincidence. Too often coincidence translated to a threat still in hiding. And for some unknown reason, Darcy was the target.

Chapter 6

"There are no coincidences in this business." Kneeling to check the door lock for jimmied scratch marks, Max spoke over his shoulder to Lurch—known to the rest of the world as Captain Rick DeMassi. "Rule number three for undercover work, right, Perry?"

"You got it, boss." Perry swept his hand along picture frames searching for bugs—the electrical, listening kind this time.

"Yeah, yeah, whatever," DeMassi chanted. The Special Operations pararescueman assigned to oversee physical safety reached up into the light fixture to feel for openings. Hopefully, the guy would never have to serve in his primary capacity for this mission—dragging someone out of the water if the op turned sour. "But I'm telling you, I was watchin' the place, keeping an eye out for Renshaw, too, like you...*requested.*

Easy enough since you're two doors down. I'm telling you, no one went in or out from eight until now.''

The CIA hadn't spared any expense in tapping the best resources of the joint services Special Operations Forces.

As much as Max chafed at accounting to others, he had to admit DeMassi seemed to know his job. The guy managed inconspicuous well, especially for an oversize New York-Italian in Guam.

Max skimmed a finger along the hinges of the door to the next room, but no fresh wood showed to indicate the hinges had been taken off and replaced. ''Then somehow it came in earlier.''

Darcy had been locked in tight and alone with the snake lying in wait. Frustrated anger spiked. He needed the reassurance that he could hold someone accountable, nail that person to the wall and make damned certain no more *coincidences* happened on his watch. ''Perry, check the housecleaning roster. I want to know who serviced this room today.''

''Will do.'' The assistant jotted a note in his day-runner with one hand, loosening his bow tie with the other. He tugged it free and draped it over his sports jacket hanging on a chair.

Max stepped up onto the bed and tapped the ceiling. Solid cinder block like the walls, built to withstand typhoons. Nothing had slithered in that way.

DeMassi's arms bulged through the openings of his sleeveless T-shirt as he twisted a screwdriver along an air-conditioning vent. Finally he dropped his hands to his side with a huff. ''Nothing came in through those.'' He raked a finger along the outside. ''And the dust is so damned thick and undisturbed you can file a complaint with the cleaning staff when you get that name.''

Max stepped back to the floor and knelt beside the bed, trying not to think about Darcy sprawled on the floor earlier. A tough-as-hell proposition when her baby powder scent clung to the sheet trailing off the side.

He didn't even bother trying to control the urge to protect her. Hell, it would be weeks before he could suppress the image of that snake inches from her face.

Dropping to his side, Max peered underneath the bed. He snagged his gun and tucked it in his waist holster before looking again. More dust and shadows. He reached a hand out behind him. ''Hey, DeMassi, pass me a flashlight.''

The flashlight smacked into his palm. Max swung the beam under the bed. A long swath sliced through the dust, a clear coil pattern in the middle. A damned big coil.

Max whipped upright before the anger could twist any tighter. ''At least we know where the thing hid out. But then, who the hell knows how long it slept curled under there?''

DeMassi crouched beside him. ''It could have slithered past while the maids were cleaning the bathrooms.''

Max stood, scoping the room while scenarios played out in his head. ''Who's in the next room?''

Perry flipped a page in his leather planner. ''U-2 pilot from Beale AFB. She left this afternoon to head back home to California.''

Max flung the flashlight on the bed and crossed to the connecting bathroom. A possibility.

Returning to Darcy's room, Max paced while Perry

worked the crank on the hurricane shutters. Restless energy without an outlet fueled Max's feet. "I'm not sold on the coincidence theory of two attacks in one day."

DeMassi scooped the mag-light from the bed. "The same car or guy following you twice in a day, that's no coincidence. Clicks on different phones, not a coincidence. But freaky weird animals in Guam are pretty much the norm, Doc."

Max grunted, unwilling to dismiss the possibility so quickly. Could DeMassi be an insider leak? He'd been the one following Darcy, after all, with a free and clear order to do so. The guy had opportunity to plant the pests. Seemed unlikely, but Max wasn't ruling out anything. He paused by the dresser, his hand absently flipping Post-it notes filled with Darcy's scrawl scattered along the mirror.

"Fill out mission reports."

"Check takeoff currency."

"Fly-safe meeting—O'Club—1600."

All written on pink posties with a lighter floral background—her warrior spirit mixed with undeniable femininity tempted him.

"Okay," Perry drawled, snapping shut his day-planner. "Say it's not coincidence. What's the motive for anyone messing with Renshaw?"

DeMassi reached up into the corner of the mirror and pulled down a faded family photo. "Someone's jealous of her high connections? The U-2 pilot even." He thumped the picture. "Wants to see General Renshaw's daughter screw up. Or maybe even just a practical joke. God knows those flyers are always pulling something."

"Possible," Max conceded, taking the photograph of dad, daughters and a son. Darcy wore her school uniform, all arms and legs with scabby knees and no front teeth. And a killer smile even then. "In which case it's petty stuff, nothing to do with the mission."

DeMassi flicked the photo in Max's hand. "Unless you're sleeping with her."

The memory of Darcy in skimpy ribbed cotton mocked him.

"So?" DeMassi pressed. "Are you?"

Max dropped the picture on the dresser. "No. Hell, no! This is work. Rule number one—avoid entangling alliances."

DeMassi folded his arms over his pumped chest. "Why the hell can't you Agency boys speak plain English? Say it like it is. Nothing can screw up ops for a guy faster than a woman."

Too damned true.

"Coincidence or not." Perry tapped his day-planner against his palm. "There's no way to tell now. We just have to weigh the risks of pressing on versus shutting down. At the end of the day, it's your ass on the line, Max. That makes it your call."

Perry could claim it was Max's choice all he wanted, but that didn't change the facts. They didn't have any hard evidence on the snake issue to warrant even a call to his superiors, much less stand a chance of convincing them to risk his cover by any major change of plans. "We press on."

Max rubbed his thumb over the family photo resting on the dresser and couldn't shake the edgy feeling he'd made the wrong decision. Perry and DeMassi were dead right about a woman messing with a man's mind. Particularly a woman like Darcy Renshaw. But he'd be rational tomorrow.

For tonight he intended to make sure nothing and no one else came near her.

"Sirs, you've done your duty by the wounded co-pilot," Darcy said to Bronco and Crusty as they stepped out of the rental car. Fluorescent floodlights hummed in the 2:00 a.m. silence outside the three-story VOQ. She stifled a yawn. "Enough hovering. Scat. Go play Nintendo or something."

Bronco slammed the door on the Ford Tempo, activating the locks. "Enjoy it while it lasts, Wren. Do you need help walking?"

Laughing, she backed away before Crusty or Bronco could swing her up into some embarrassing fireman's carry. "No. Thanks, really. I appreciate you driving me back from the infirmary. But I'll be fine. Even Doc Clark says so, and heaven knows flight surgeons are infamous for being hard-nosed." She turned to Bronco. "No offense to your wife."

"None taken." He winked, stopping outside her room. "Put your leg up like Cutter said and get some sleep."

"Will do, sir." She twisted the knob behind her.

Darcy waited until they climbed the outdoor staircase to the second floor, and their footsteps thudded overhead before she sagged against the tan cinderblock wall. How could a few tiny bites sting so much? Her leg throbbed like hell. Doc Clark had pumped her full of IV antibiotics and antivenom until her arm throbbed, too. Then he'd released her with instructions to keep off her leg for the night.

At least he hadn't insisted she stay in the infirmary.

How embarrassing that would have been. Forget going down in a blaze of combat glory.

She'd been grounded by a snake.

Three days DNIF—duties not including flying. Nobody dared argue with a flight surgeon's verdict. She was stuck flying a desk and passing out mission packages. Probably for the best, since she couldn't stop her hands from shaking. She just wanted to peel off her clothes and climb in the shower before she crumbled. She'd worry later about how she would fall asleep again.

Darcy trailed a finger down the splintered wooden frame until her hand steadied.

A Renshaw warrior shows no fear.

Darcy tossed her shoulders back and plowed inside.

"Bet you can't name everyone from *Gilligan's Island*."

Darcy spun on her heel. Max lounged in a chair tucked in a corner behind the door. One leg slung lazily over the arm of the chair, the other stretched out. His sea-foam windbreaker was zipped halfway up his chest, clashing magnificently with his pineapple-patterned bathing suit.

"Actors or characters?" She reached behind her to close the door—and give herself time to slow her heartbeat.

"You've had a helluva night, so I'll let you off easy with naming the characters."

A simple, shared smile and the room closed in on her with warm intimacy. The jean shorts and T-shirt she'd yanked on over her ribbed tank and panties before going to the infirmary might as well have faded away. Max's gaze cruised a slow ride from her face all the way to her sandals. Those blue-green eyes held full knowledge of how little she'd been wearing earlier.

He'd noticed.

He hadn't forgotten.

And he liked what he saw.

Darcy forced herself to meet Max's probing gaze dead-on. No more backing down for her tonight. She scavenged for a smile and steady steps as she closed the space between them. Leaning against the table beside him, she crossed her ankles unobtrusively to ease the pressure on her leg. "Gilligan, Skipper, Professor, Mary Ann, Ginger and the Howells. To damn easy. Next time, no quarter, Doc. I can hold my own."

"Fair enough. Renshaw scores, winning back her gun." Max lifted a hand from his thigh to reveal her Beretta.

Damn. How the hell had she forgotten it?

He flipped it to hold by the barrel and passed it to her, handle first.

"Thanks." She tested the reassuring weight of her military issue Beretta M-9, the grip still warm from his touch. "The security police weren't too happy with me for discharging my weapon in the VOQ."

An understatement. But then the Base Commander had strutted into the infirmary interview and—surprise, surprise—smoothed things over for the daughter of his old friend Hank Renshaw. Darcy ground her teeth against a fresh kick of frustration over special treatment she didn't want or deserve.

Max nudged aside a shell casing on the floor. "Good thing you were on the first story in a corner room or someone could have caught a stray shot."

"I never miss." She took comfort in the familiar weight.

"Everyone misses sometimes."

"Not me." She pointed the gun away, pushed the

release and ejected the clip. "I got my first gun for my fourteenth birthday. A Colt Woodsman, twenty-two caliber. Some fathers like Bronco take their kids to the zoo. Mine took me to the shooting range."

The General, then the Colonel, had wanted to make damned sure his little girl could defend herself next time trouble tried to snatch her away. He'd trained her well.

Darcy switched the gun to her other hand, slid back the action, locked and cleared the chamber. The familiar ritual soothed her tattered nerves.

Nope. She hadn't worried about missing. Once she'd remembered her gun in her bag by the bed, she'd known she could take out the snake. If only she could have done it faster.

Bile burned her throat.

Darcy turned away from Max's prying eyes. She scooped up her flight bag from the floor and sank to the edge of the bed before her knees gave out. She tucked her gun inside. "Thanks for charging to the rescue."

"No problem."

"Your method for handling the snake worked much better than mine." *Breathe in. Breathe out.*

The past and present melded at a time when her defenses registered somewhere between nil and non-existent. Max's voice echoed in her head with a far-away timbre.

"Local pest control will probably thank us either way, since the tree snakes have all but wiped out the bird population on Guam."

"It must have heard my call sign is Wren."

She blinked back the memory of a dirty hand draping a snake over her shoulders and reminding her that good girls listened. Good girls also didn't try to give hints about her captors during a phone call to her father.

Darcy swallowed. Hard. She had thirty seconds, tops, to get Max out of the room before she hurled. "I don't mean to sound ungrateful, but could you go now? I'm past ready to sleep."

Footsteps sounded just before Max eased into sight, kneeling in front of her. "I wanted to make sure you're okay before I turn in."

"As you can see, I'm all right." Four valuable seconds passed and still his fine butt stayed in her room. *Twenty seconds left.*

"Call me if you start feeling any ill effects from the bites."

She nodded tightly, her mouth firmly closed.

Fifteen.

She would not disgrace herself by tossing her supper on this guy's Teva sandals. With her luck today, the flyers would all pour back out into the hall, and she'd be stuck with a call sign like "Ralph" for the rest of her career.

"Okay, then. I'll let you get some sleep." Max stood. "But remember. Call if you need anything."

"Just listen for the warning shots in the air, *Gunsmoke* style."

Laughing softly, he pulled the door shut behind him. Leaving her alone with the rumpled bed and memories of fangs sinking into her flesh.

Darcy pressed a hand to her churning stomach and sprinted for the bathroom. Later she would ask Max why a marine biologist had been carrying a Glock 29 when he'd kicked his way into her room.

* * *

Standing on the deserted walkway outside Darcy's VOQ room, Max adjusted his Glock in the waist harness under his windbreaker and wondered what he was missing. She seemed her normal tough-as-nails self, taking the snakebite in stride. A slightly limping stride, sure, but better than ninety-nine percent of the world would have handled an attack from a ten-foot reptile.

Still, something didn't sit right about the way she'd shuffled him out. The shadows under her eyes hinted at more than exhaustion. He would know. He lived in those shadows himself.

He should leave before someone came out to find him hanging around her door. And he *would* go, as soon as he heard the new dead bolt click.

Two interminable minutes later, it still hadn't slid into place. Didn't the woman have any safety sense?

Max rapped his knuckles on the frame twice. "Darcy, I think my, uh—" he scrambled "—zinc oxide fell out of my pocket."

Smooth line, slick. No wonder she didn't answer. He tapped again. The door creaked open. "Darcy?"

He scanned the empty room.

"Over here."

Max followed her voice across the room…and down to the bathroom floor. Damn it, he should have trusted his instincts earlier and never left.

She slumped back against the wall, her knees drawn to her chest. Pale but upright, she reached to flush. "Shut the door, please. I really don't want anyone else seeing me like this."

"You got it." Max closed the door before crossing to Darcy. Stepping over her, he snagged a washrag from the rack and soaked it with cold water. Darcy thrust her hand up. Max passed the rag down as he dropped beside her on the cool tile. "Do you need anything?"

Darcy mopped the cloth over her brow. "A new day would be nice."

"How about I get someone to stay with you?"

"No!" She swiped the rag over her eyes. "No. Just what I need, Crusty waving a bologna sandwich under my nose to make all my troubles go away." She shuddered. "I'd never live it down. It's tough enough proving myself to these guys as it is."

"What about one of the other women?"

"No. I don't want anyone here." Darcy shot him a pointed look. "*Anyone.* I've had a really sucky day. So please find your zinc oxide and leave."

Hiking up onto her knees, Darcy grabbed the toothpaste from the sink. She fell back on her bottom. She squirted a stream of mint gel on her finger and swiped it across her teeth, all the while carefully avoiding looking at him.

Max clasped his hands loosely between his knees. "There's nothing wrong with being rattled by what went down here."

Darcy pitched the toothpaste in the sink. "If you're thinking about rolling out a story of how you once ralphed after facing a shark, don't bother. It won't make me feel any less embarrassed."

In spite of her bravado, he figured she could do without his Mako shark story, or the jagged reminder on his hip. And he could never tell her the top-secret details about how he'd received the scar on his shoulder.

Max pointed to two pin-size scars on his calf instead. "Actually, it was a sea snake, the first time I

came to Guam. Just a juvenile one.'' Lucky for him
since an adult sea snake could open its jaw wide
enough to span a table. Max exhaled long and slow.
''I don't care how long you've been working in the
water, those are scary mothers. Damned thing got
ahold of my leg and wouldn't let go.''

His muscles had stiffened up within a half hour, his
jaw locking. He'd have died without the antivenom,
but she didn't need that much detail. ''There's nothing
wrong with being scared into worshipping the porce-
lain god over there as long as you don't let the fear
immobilize you when it counts.''

''That's not my point.'' She stopped, bit her lip,
shook her head before continuing, ''I shouldn't expect
you would understand about my job. We're just from
two different walks of life.'' She nudged his foot with
hers. ''But then I guess the different-worlds part is a
lot of what I enjoy about you, Dr. Maxwell Keagan.''

There it was again. The reality that Darcy would
make a military sharp turn in the other direction if she
knew the truth about him. He should be relieved. He
wasn't.

She scooped the rag off the floor and flung it in the
sink with the toothpaste. ''Thanks for checking on me.
Twice. But I'm better now. I should put my leg up
and go to sleep so I can finally call this day over.''

She studied the bed as if it were a hill to conquer,
a battle to win. He couldn't just walk out and leave
her alone with those demons lurking behind her eyes.

And maybe he needed a little while longer to reassure himself the snake was nothing more than coincidence after all.

Without taking time to think and therefore change
his mind, Max scooped her up in his arms. Darcy

yelped, flinging her arms around his neck. "What are you doing?"

Turning sideways, he angled out of the bathroom. "You need to stay off your feet, and I've got an idea for the perfect place to do that."

"Uh, Max." She eyed the bed. "I don't need you to tuck me in."

"That's good. Because you're not going to bed." Not there anyway.

"I'm not inviting you to keep me awake either."

An image he did *not* need, thank you very much, especially with her nestled so warm and soft against him. "I'm not offering. I prefer my bed partners not be half-dead on their feet."

She needed a distraction and he intended to provide one. He refused to question his impulsive decision. He dipped to twist open the knob and toed the door open. Staying away from her hadn't kept her safe, and he'd already determined he couldn't shut down the investigation. Which left him only one alternative. Keep Darcy with him whenever possible.

Starting now.

"Max!" She slapped a hand to the door frame to stop him from moving farther. "I'm not so sure whatever you have planned is such a good idea."

Securing her against his chest, he stared into her shadowed brown eyes and asked, "Are you really ready to try sleeping?"

Her hand slid from the door frame and curled around his neck. "Where are we going?"

"To find some neutral ground."

Chapter 7

Neutral ground? Being held in Max's arms seemed more like landing smack-dab in the middle of an explosive mine field. Darcy stayed rock still as Max carried her along the outdoor walkway.

The man was hung up on another woman, for crying out loud.

Darcy tried to ignore the scent of musk and suntan oil. Tried. And failed. Damn it, she didn't need the grief of wanting a guy who wanted someone else. Especially not now when her emotional reserves lodged somewhere in the negative numbers after the whole snake debacle.

Max rounded the corner, tucking her closer, nestling her breasts against his buff chest. Her traitorous body responded. Please, Lord, she hoped Max wouldn't notice.

She wasn't sure how much more of his TLC she could withstand before she lost it. Except he'd nailed her state of mind dead-on in guessing she couldn't stomach staying confined to her room. The night air and Max's arms surrounding her made for a fabulous sensory distraction. "How far away is this neutral ground of yours?"

"Not much farther." He jostled her closer, launching a shower of tingles from his touch all the way to the roots of her windswept hair.

"Good. Because while I appreciate the ride, I'm not overly anxious to be dropped."

"No worries." Hot, muscled strength rippled through his arms, against her skin, confirming his claim of a strength that could carry her for miles. For hours. Long, satisfying hours.

Max started up the outdoor stairs. Stairs? Darcy eyed the sunning deck on the roof over the center section of the cinder-block VOQ. At two in the morning, the cement expanse sprawled blessedly empty but for the call of night creatures and the whisper of salty wind.

Without breaking stride or a sweat, he cleared the steps and kicked wide the metal gate. White plastic lawn chairs and recliners were scattered over the deck, tables interspersed. Max strode toward two recliners nearest the fence and lowered Darcy into one.

His arms slid from beneath her slowly, gently. The night blanketed her with intoxicating heat. Maybe her body only hummed from all the meds or adrenaline rather than arousal. Either way, her skin burned everywhere he touched.

Parking-lot lights and the moon showered a nimbus through the whitened spikes of Max's hair, begging her fingers to explore. Just as she started to surrender and raise her hand, Max settled onto a chair beside her and propped his feet on the rail with his typical negligent ease that dominated any landscape he occupied.

What was it about him that drew her so? Already she knew she wouldn't forget him or their time together on the island. She hated unresolved business, like the way the lingering fears from her kidnapping had been brought too sharply into focus tonight.

Now Max was quickly gaining an importance in her life that wouldn't be easily dismissed. And that worried her.

Time to find out more about him. With any luck he would admit to something majorly piggish in his past, which would launch him into the realms of jerkdom and out of her mind.

Yeah, right. "Thanks for what you did earlier."

"No big deal." He kept his face forward, eyes narrowed and focused on the darkened expanse of island and sea in front of them. "I'm sure you would have finished off the snake on your own."

"I meant later. Checking on me." Darcy tore her gaze from him and stared out into the night. The hazy glow of spotlights illuminated a museum-quality B-52 on static display. "Thank God I didn't bring Crusty or one of the other guys back to my room. They would have razzed the hell out of me for years over finding you there."

Max's jaw flexed. "I knew you wouldn't ask them for help. That's why I stayed."

"Oh." Gulp. Already this guy had her number. So much for being an Alicia-style enigma.

Of course Alicia had told her on the phone earlier to cut herself some slack. A trip to Guam for Darcy had to be as tough as flying combat mission over Cantou from the cockpit of an F-15.

Yeah, right. She wasn't buying it then and wasn't buying it now. She felt compelled to offer Max an explanation for her meltdown so he wouldn't think she was a weak-kneed twit. "When I was a kid here on Guam, I was—" she paused to find a word that worked while still hiding the truth she wasn't ready to share, especially not tonight "—I got lost in the jungle. I had some bad experiences with those Guam critters before my father, uh, found me a few days later on Lovers' Leap cliff."

Max's eyes shone with quiet empathy as if he somehow understood the rest without her even having to tell him. "That would be tough for a kid. Even for an adult."

"It was. Especially being stuck there with that creepy legend about two doomed lovers jumping to their death rather than let the girl be married off to some Spanish soldier. I mean, damn. Why didn't they both just paddle to another island? Fight back?"

Of course she'd been to Guam since the kidnapping yet hadn't strayed more than a few yards from base. Her leg throbbed. "Of course who am I to talk? I should probably just go confront my fears. Hike through those jungles and even up to the cliff. Conquer my mountain."

Max straightened. "You don't have to face those critters alone, you know. Call me. I'll take that hike with you, be an extra set of eyes to watch out for…more tree snakes."

Her heartbeat tripped over itself. Oh, man. She was in serious trouble.

Darcy looked away before his sea-green eyes had

her plunging right into their sympathetic depths and into those strong arms. She stared out over the moon-speckled water to the dim glow from the island of Rhoda. No one in sight. Safe, for now.

Of course she could take care of herself—wouldn't rely on the protection of others ever again. Twelve years ago, she'd been snacking on a plate of roasted poi on the wide-open beach with a hundred partying Air Force warriors around her. Still she'd been snatched.

These days she preferred the metal-encased protection of her aircraft and her own defenses. "Thanks. I'll keep your offer in mind."

Alicia would be proud of her elusive answer. Too bad it had more to do with self-preservation than enticement.

"Don't you feel exposed out here?" Darcy picked at her sweaty T-shirt and tried not to think of how little she'd been wearing earlier.

"I can see anyone coming long before they get anywhere near me. No chance for one of life's ambushes."

Ah, a kindred spirit. "No snakes under your bed, huh?"

"I guess you could say that." Max folded his hands over his washboard stomach. "I like the wide-open space and the quiet. It's almost as good as being underwater."

She'd never considered that his diving could be a way to achieve ultimate solitude—which made his taking time to comfort her all the more special.

Special. A shiver of longing prickled. Dangerous when she was so vulnerable.

Silence settled, steamy, heavy. Needy. Darcy

searched for something to fill the space between them so she wouldn't fall victim to the temptation to explore the muscles cutting his chest.

She pointed to the spotlit plane. "My dad flew that in when the other B-52 monument blew off the blocks during a hurricane." She kept her eyes fixed ahead. "I assume you know who my father is?"

Max blinked but didn't turn to her. "Hank Renshaw? General rumored to be next in line for Chairman of the Joint Chiefs of Staff? Yeah, I've heard of him."

"Who hasn't, right?" She forced a laugh. Her father's prestige and power had brought about the kidnapping. Not that she blamed him. Her old man blamed himself enough for fifty people. "When Dad pulled his stint here as the Squadron Commander, crewdogs painted over all the signs that carried his name and title. They replaced it with 'Uncle Hank: Best Damned Bomber Pilot in the United States Air Force.'"

Darcy stared out at the plane. She'd been certain her indomitable father would wing in to the rescue. He had. But it had taken so damned long. "Sometimes I wish I'd felt the calling to be an artist. Or a lawyer. Or a teacher. Something different from my old man." A job where the memories wouldn't dog her.

"But the genes run too strong."

She nodded, surprised he understood. "Exactly. I have to fly. It's like breathing for me. Except my father owns all the air." Her fighter pilot sister had figured out how to make it work and her bomber brother just didn't care.

Why the hell wasn't there a patch of the sky she

could claim for her own? Not one she'd located yet, anyway. "I wish I could find my niche in his world."

Sharing her frustrations felt good. Max was so easy to talk to, a good listener. No games. No facades. Just open honesty. "I feel as if I have ten times more to prove to these guys because of the Air Force pedigree. I need to make sure everyone knows I earned my wings with hard work instead of soaking up the benefits of nepotism."

She smacked her throbbing leg in frustration. "Damn it, I should be flying combat in Cantou instead of working the Flipper Flight." Darcy stopped short. "Uh, no offense."

A half smile tipped a dimple into Max's cheek. "None taken."

"Of course, now I can't even fly in earthquake relief supplies for three days. My missions will have to be taken on by someone else. Way to make a big impression as the new co around the squadron."

Max turned solemn eyes her way. "The crew's respect for you seems rock solid."

His sure tone bolstered her. Typical for the guy— minimal words, maximum punch.

"I hope so. Trust in the air is everything, and I need to know they trust me to hold up my end flying. That I'm a wingman to be counted on."

Pausing midramble, Darcy glanced over at Max. This man had a way of making her babble on about herself and things she didn't really want to talk about anyway. She could almost see Alicia shooting her a mocking yawn symbol. "What about you? Brothers? Sisters? Red-brick, middle-class America upbringing?"

He sat silently for so long she thought he might not

answer. Had she bored him to sleep after all? And if she climbed right over to him, would that stir him?

Or was he awake and she'd pushed this silent man too far?

Max shifted in his chair, eyes still half-open. "Only child. My old man was active duty—a Navy Captain. My mother and I followed him around the world."

Darcy thought of her own mother, a woman she didn't even remember except from pictures, since she'd died of an aneurysm twenty years ago. Would her mother have been able to put the kidnapping into a sharper focus? Darcy shrugged off the notion. She was doing fine on her own, damn it. "So you get your love for the water from your father."

A furrow creased his brow. "I guess so. Although he would probably choke on his commission to hear we have anything in common. I haven't been the ideal son."

With a few clipped sentences Max relayed much— a veritable sharefest for such a closemouthed man. A heady rush of success filled her. "Ah, come on. I'm sure he loves pineapples."

Max snorted.

She wanted to see his smile and bring back the rare chattiness she'd only just begun to enjoy with him. "I'll bet your clothes made for some interesting times around your house."

His eyes slid from the horizon. A surprise spark of laughter lit the edges of a smile. "And I've become conservative in my old age."

Their laughs twined. She wanted to twine a lot more with this guy.

The common bond in their upbringing only made him tougher to resist. Chitchat wasn't helping. She needed distance fast before she crawled across the deck and into his arms again.

Darcy knew just the question guaranteed to chill the heat humming through her. "So, Max, what's a marine biologist with a penchant for wild dive shorts doing packing a Glock 29 on my airplane?"

Tension ripped through Max. His every muscle tightened with a reminder to keep his guard up around this woman. He should have kept his yap shut. Instead, he'd thought it would be safe to spill a few truths about his past to relax her.

Darcy Renshaw was about as far from safe and relaxing as a man could get.

He'd screwed up and lost focus. Now he had to haul himself out of the mess and protect his cover. "My work takes me all around the world, some parts not as safe as others. I always carry a weapon."

Her eyes showered sparks his way. "You're supposed to declare that weapon before setting foot on any aircraft." She swung her legs over the side of the lounger and sat upright to pin him with an accusing glare. "I could have you thrown in jail."

Now there was an image to tempt a man—Darcy slapping cuffs on him while wearing her skimpy ribbed underwear. "I did declare it. To Daniel Baker." Max stabbed a finger toward her injured leg. "Now put your foot back up or I'll have Doc Clark lock *you* up in the infirmary."

She didn't budge. "Why Crusty?"

"He's the senior pilot."

Max watched her mull that over until the will to argue seeped out of her set shoulders. A momentary retreat, no doubt, but welcome.

"Okay, then." She reclined back and swung her

legs onto the lounger. "Next time, I'd advise telling all the aircrew or you could land yourself in trouble."

"I'll keep that in mind." How pissed would she be if she found out the rest of what had been kept from her? She made it clear she didn't appreciate back-seat roles, but life didn't always offer choices.

He had a job to do and a woman to protect. And he damned well didn't intend to let her wander off alone into the jungle to face her childhood ghosts and present day "critters." Whether she wanted it or not, this woman had his protection.

A woman mellowing into a sleepy haze. Her body lolled, relaxed, sagging into a seductive sprawl on the lounger that sent heat rushing south with throbbing intensity.

Max speared a hand through his hair, scanning the perimeter from his higher vantage point. What would it be like to make love to this uninhibited woman out in the open? She might be innocent, but he recognized a sensualist when he saw one. And Darcy was one hell of an enthusiastic sensualist. It would be a lucky man who tapped into that.

Hell. He did not need jealousy burning his gut. She wasn't his and never would be.

Waves lapped in the distance with a lulling regularity. Darcy's eyelids drifted closed, her breathing rhythmic.

Finally Max allowed himself the pleasure of looking at her—so damned pretty. Not gorgeous in some unapproachable-model kind of way, but pretty. Real. And alive, thank God.

In the quiet and solitude of the night, Max let himself say the words he'd bottled up for hours. "You scared the hell out of me with those gunshots. It knocked a year off my life seeing you on the floor with that snake.''

A smile teased at the corner of her lips, her lashes still caressing her cheeks. ''I told you. I never miss.''

Sighing, she nestled on her side, cheek on her hand.

She didn't miss? Well, neither did he. And he knew it would be tougher than he'd thought keeping his hands off her while ensuring she didn't fall victim to any more ''coincidences.''

Darcy pulled herself through at least seven layers of sleepy fog. She turned her face into the pillow. A pillow. Not a lawn chair. Sometime during the night, Max must have carried her back to her room.

She'd actually slept through the chance to snuggle against that muscle-cut chest again. She must have been more wasted than she'd thought. Probably for the best as she would have been tempted to pull him down onto the covers with her to discover if he had other tattoos.

To uncover more pieces of Max's past.

Darcy arched into a languorous stretch. Her leg throbbed from the bites, just as her mind throbbed with memories of moonlight and Max. She didn't want to leave the bed and lose the dreamtime with him that had so perfectly overlaid the horror from earlier.

She'd found more distraction than she'd bargained for with the hunky professor. Sure, the night glow and solitude had been sexy, but the talking had been even more intimate. Somehow confusingly different from the friendships she shared with her crewdog buddies.

None of them could have pried bits of those past Guam days out of her. Yet wasn't this trip about putting that time behind her? She wrestled with lending too much importance to her sharing with Max.

Tougher than wrestling a ten-foot snake.

As difficult as putting her past behind her.

Of course, so far she'd made zero progress in that department, too. One little encounter with a tree snake and she'd been plunged back into that nightmare time.

Get a grip, soldier.

Darcy rolled out of bed. She tested her weight on her injured calf. Winced. Wincing even more at the next three days she would spend working a desk in the squadron until she returned to flying status. Might as well get to it.

Today would be as good a time as any to start confronting those critter memories with a hike to stretch out her tension kinks. She limped over to her dresser. The scraggly, puffy-eyed image in the mirror mocked her. No wonder Max kept his distance. She grabbed a brush and started yanking it through her tangled rat's nest of hair.

Darcy paused midstroke. One of her flowered sticky notes waited on the mirror. She dropped her brush beside her day-planner and peeled the paper from the mirror.

''Meet us at the bay—6:00 p.m. Lucy and Ethel.''

Anticipation, too much, stung her stomach as she remembered his insistence from the night before that he accompany her on her jungle walks. She crumpled the pink Post-It note in her fist. Damn Max Keagan and his mixed signals. Sit with me on the deck, but don't touch me. Stay away. Come see me.

What did he want from her?

And what did *she* want from this man? She had friends. She wanted him to be something more, no question, but not while he carted around baggage from a dead lover.

Opening her fist, Darcy stared down at the mangled scrap of paper from a man who'd known she wouldn't want to be alone but had let her keep her pride. A man who called few people friends, but had been there for her. Somehow, just talking to him had hauled her through a hellish night. Maybe he could pull her through the next weeks confronting her past as well.

Darcy placed the paper on her dresser and slowly smoothed out the wrinkles until it lay flat again.

No, she wasn't sure what she wanted from Max anymore. But she knew she would be sorry if she left the island before finding out.

Max eased his boat into the bay. The sight of Darcy waiting for him had become familiar over the past two weeks, since he'd issued the initial invitation to join him. An invitation to keep her safe had somehow turned into something else.

Today she'd chosen the dock rather than a sandbar, sitting on the edge with her feet dangling in the surf. Her black suit clung to her honey-tanned body, dog tags dangling from her neck. Between her breasts.

He forced his hungry eyes up. Her welcoming smile blazed brighter than the tropical sun toasting his back.

A rare thing for him, a welcome-home scenario, and yet he'd become too accustomed to it in a few short weeks. Darcy waited while he moored the boat. Sometimes she met Perry and him at the dolphin pen. Other times she waited at the boat launch. Just for him.

He'd always been a loner. His animals made more loyal companions than people, anyway. They also had fewer expectations, a corner of his brain taunted.

Yet Darcy never asked anything of him. Just that he hang with her. No great hardship, hanging with Darcy Renshaw in her bathing suit.

Sometime during the past days things had gone from professional to personal. He and Darcy had scoured nearly every inch of the island together. Whatever ghosts waited for her there, she faced them, shadows lurking in her eyes.

He knew the basics about her kidnapping from her file, not that she'd ever confided in him. At least the "critter coincidences" had stopped, but he couldn't convince himself to back away. He was just being cautious.

Yeah, right, chump.

And in another few days she would be returning home. His stint as her unknown guardian would be over and he could forge ahead with finishing his mission.

Damn, but that sandbar and dock would be empty. More so than before. He would miss talking to her. Miss that he'd never had the chance to peel her suit off.

Miss her.

"Hey there, Keagan," his personal siren called, waving as she pulled her feet from the water. "About time you showed up."

How long did it take to draw a pair of never-ending legs from the water?

Finally she stood and swiped beads of water from her tanned skin.

Max swallowed and concentrated on docking the boat rather than parking himself in Darcy. "Busy day."

One that left him itching. He was so damned close

to locating that tap. He could feel the logic pattern of which cable contained it gel in his mind. He knew. But until he had solid proof, the knowledge was useless to his superiors. He'd run Lucy and Ethel up and down the cable four times with no luck. What was he missing?

He couldn't afford wasted time with operatives in the field and crews flying missions over Cantou. Darcy's words on the VOQ roof after the snake attack came back to haunt him. How she wanted to be in the action in Cantou. The edge of urgency to plug that damned leak upped tenfold.

Soon, he reassured himself. Soon. Then the real maneuvering would begin in the dance of filtered misinformation to flush out the traitor. He counted the hours until Darcy's departure took her away and safe. Took her away. Period.

Damn it. He couldn't afford to regret her leaving.

The tide drew the boat closer, engine in idle gurgling water behind. With a familiarity two weeks in the making, he pitched her the line to tie off the boat.

She looped it around her hand but didn't move to secure the craft. "Get your party Tevas on, Doc. Crewdogs are throwing a farewell luau on the base beach. It's sure to be hokey and full of food, just like the 'Brady Bunch Goes to Hawaii' episode."

He wanted to go with her. Too much. "Thanks, but I'll have to pass. Stacks of paperwork."

She perched a hand on her hip. "So don't sleep tonight. Time's awasting, and I'll be leaving soon. There'll be ukulele solos by torchlight. More shish kebabs than you can eat in two lifetimes. You don't even have to talk to us humans if you don't want. God knows, no one can get a word in edgewise around Bronco and Crusty, anyway.''

Or around her, either, but damn she was mesmerizing to listen to and watch.

Darcy inched closer. ''At least give me a ride over. I'm still too wasted from yesterday's flight to hike back to base,'' she groused, her body screaming a vitality that mocked her claims of weakness.

He hesitated.

She scrunched her nose. ''If you don't come, Bronco's going to pair me up with that new copilot. The big lug is so happily married he thinks everyone should invest in a ring and make a pack of Kodak memories. Pretend to be my date and protect me from that overgrown Cupid.''

Protect. The single word reminded him of his need to keep her clear of a lot more than that. ''When you put it that way, how can I say no to you?''

''You can't.''

No damn kidding.

Darcy stepped onto the nose of his boat and tossed the line back to him. Her water shoes slid along the slick deck. Max steadied her. Hands to her waist, careful to keep a safe distance, he lifted her into the boat, steeling himself to keep his distance. As if the tempting give of womanly flesh under his hands wasn't already tempting him to throw away rational thoughts.

A traitorous wave slapped the boat. Darcy pitched into his arms.

Ah, hell. Warm, wet Darcy molded to him, every inch of him. Every throbbing, too-damn-long-denied, starving inch of him that was fed up with keeping her at arm's length.

He wanted to tangle their bodies together on the

floor of the boat, strip away bathing suits and inhibitions. Screw the job. Screw being honorable. Just…screw everything until they both couldn't breathe.

Hell, he couldn't breathe now.

His hands tightened around her waist just as her breasts tightened against his skin. He wished he'd put on a shirt. He knew it wouldn't have made any difference.

Her full breasts beaded against his chest. Branded him. Her generous lips parted, lips as generous as the woman. It would be so easy to take from her.

Confusion flickered through her eyes just before she plastered on an overbright smile and stepped back. Damn, it took forever for her to peel herself away.

Okay, maybe five seconds. Might as well have been five hours for all the torture he endured.

"All righty, Doc." Darcy's thready voice drifted along the air as she made her way around a cooler of bottled water. "Let's fire up this boat and hit the beach before Crusty eats all the food." She plopped down in the passenger seat, swiping a strand of hair from her brow.

Her hands shook.

He was an ass. He'd done this, sent her confusing signals until this honest, good—totally hot—woman didn't know how to react. She deserved open emotion, and, hell yes, open desire from a guy who had something more to give her than a dried-up heart and rootless life.

But damned if he would let her find that guy tonight.

Max stepped behind the wheel of the boat and kicked it into reverse, backing away from the dock with more speed than necessary thanks to the frustration fueling his every move. Water chugged from the engine, then quieted as he guided the boat forward, chopping through the waves. Darcy stretched her legs on the side of the boat to absorb dwindling rays. If the woman glowed any more, he would be blinded.

He pulled his attention away from her and piloted the boat along the tropical shoreline, trees darker, denser in the hazy glow of sunset. The sheer cliff of Lovers' Leap stretched in the distance, about the only landmark Darcy hadn't trekked through in the past weeks. Her confidences she'd shared on the roof echoed—how her father had found her on the cliff after the kidnapping she labeled a disappearance.

Max pointed the nose of the boat away from the site. "I guess you went to luaus before as a kid, when your dad was stationed in Guam?"

The engine hummed in the silence. He glanced at her. "Darcy?"

He looked past the outward glow and found more of those shadows in her eyes.

Then she smiled, her Darcy-glow back. "Sure did. Nobody can party like a crewdog. By the time I was thirteen, I even knew how to roast a pig with banana skins and ti leaves slapped over the carcass, burlap bags over the pit to hold in the heat." She winked. "Hope you're hungry."

This woman made him hungry for things he hadn't even known he wanted. "I'll trust your recommendation."

"Rumor has it Crusty and Doc Clark are going to pin Bronco and take pictures of him in a coconut bra to post around the squadron. I'm sure they would welcome your help holding down the big lug."

More of her attempts to socialize him. Many had tried before her…and failed. "Darcy."

"Huh?"

He guided the boat through a cut in the lurking coral reef, then sped up again. "Do you ever bother with subtle?"

"Subtle's never been my strong suit."

His hands gripped the wheel. "I appreciate your efforts to include me in your friends' flyer games. But if you wanted to hang with somebody who's at the heart of a party, you should have parked yourself in front of Crusty's room." And he was damned glad she hadn't. "This is who I am."

"Grumpy?" She softened the jab with a grin.

"Most of the time." Like now.

The boat sliced through waves, bouncing, sending showers of water up to sprinkle Darcy's skin. Cling to her lashes. "Actually, I prefer to think you just have untapped social skills."

He plastered a scowl on his face that he well knew wouldn't deter her warrior spirit in the least. "And at the moment you have untapped manners."

"Hmm." She flashed him an indomitable smile. "I've learned subtle and polite don't work with you."

He grunted.

She swung her legs from the side of the boat. Elbows on her knees, she leaned toward him. "I figured something out these past couple of weeks. You need to smile more often, Max Keagan."

"And you've decided it's your personal mission to make that happen with luaus and coconut bras?"

Memories of Eva scratched at his mind, of her trying to tease a smile from him. She would have liked Darcy.

The thought bothered him. A lot.

"What are friends for?"

Max yanked his mind back to the present as they circled round a jungle cliff and into a cove. A bonfire flickered up toward to the sky. Eyeing the hundred or so military personnel gathered along the beach, he decided she wouldn't need his protection.

He cut the engine before it could chew sand and let the boat drift only feet from the beach. "My smiles are about used up for the day, Darcy. I'm going to head on back." He forced himself to say, "I'm sure any one of the crew will give you a ride home. I won't be good company tonight."

"No one's asking you to be." Darcy braced her hand on the dash. "You don't have to play. You don't even have to smile. Just roll out one of those frowns of yours and eat. You have to eat, you know, as much as you seem resistant to admitting you're mortal like the rest of us. So come on. Luau means feast, and I am more than ready to pig out."

Her hand clenched around the dash until her knuckles whitened. "Please, Max. I don't want to go alone."

Shadows dimmed the glow in her eyes again. There was no mistaking them this time, even in the neon haze of the drooping sun.

Darcy wore her independence like a second uniform. No doubt she could conquer whatever shadows waited on that beach for her. But she'd communicated a need for him tonight far stronger than when a snake had poised ready to strike her. He might not know why this indomitable woman needed him.

But damned if he could turn away.

"Okay, Darcy, you've got yourself a grumpy, antisocial date."

Chapter 8

Darcy leaned back against her date's bare arm. Bonfire flames licked toward the sky while she tried her damnedest to resist the temptation to lick the sweat from Max's tattoo.

Well, she'd wanted a distraction tonight from memories of another luau twelve years ago. She'd found her distraction in spades. Or rather in one hunkish guy lounging half-naked in parrot-patterned swim trunks. Thanks to Max, she'd enjoyed herself. Memories of that long-ago luau lurked but didn't overpower her.

The pig pit crackled off to the side. The remains of a carcass and a few stray sweet potatoes still smoked mouthwatering scents into the ocean breeze. Darcy shuffled her attention to the crewdogs blending together in a mesh of khakis shorts, bland swimsuits and bad Hawaiian shirts. The cluster of aircrew members was mostly comprised of the deployed contingent from McChord. But in the tight C-17 community, she knew their faces anyway.

Live music mingled with the waves in an impromptu concert. Hunkered down on the sand, Lieutenant Bo Rokowsky plucked out a Clapton classic on the guitar while Cutter wailed along about Layla.

Darcy threw herself into the semblance of normalcy, all the while too aware of undercurrents tugging her with dangerous power—toward Max. He had acted the attentive, albeit quiet, boyfriend as promised. His arm draped around her shoulders. Did he know he was playing with the chain on her dog tags? God, it seemed so intimate, the way her dog tags trailed up and down between her breasts with each tug to the chain.

They'd become friends the past weeks, a friendship marked by a definite physical distance. No touching. Until the brief, too-hot moment in his boat earlier.

Tonight there was so much touching she was beginning to believe in moonburns.

Darcy guzzled her fruity drink and let herself mellow into the light buzz humming through her, nothing compared to the full-blown buzz from Max's touch.

Think of something else. "How's it going with Lucy and Ethel? Is Lucy feeling better?"

Max's knuckle rested against the sensitive curve of her neck. "Perry adjusted her diet. She's back up to speed now."

"Good." Darcy's eyes gravitated to Max's preppy assistant.

Perry lounged against a palm tree while talking to Bronco. Coconut bra dangling from around the big lug's neck, Bronco grabbed an umbrella drink from a muumuu-clad matron passing out beverages and leis.

Personnel from the O'Club and base dive shop catered the event, a mother and son duo.

"So you'll be taking both Lucy and Ethel out to-morrow?"

"Uh-huh."

That enigmatic, heavy-lidded stare of his made her long to shock it off. And wouldn't he be shocked wide-eyed if he knew what she longed to do with the drawstring on his swim trunks?

Stop.

If the guy wanted her, he knew where to find her. She needed to respect his boundaries—and find some for herself before she unknotted that string with her teeth. "Perry will be helping you?"

Max nodded.

"Diving in teams, right?"

He grunted a yes. The dog tags traced slowly down the inside curve of her breast. She shivered.

Darcy tipped her head up to him, her face close to his. The scent of coconut and musk and man filled her already fuzzy senses. "Hey, Max?"

"Yeah, Darcy?"

"Thanks for playing your date role so well."

"No problem."

She wanted to say much more. Like thanks for un-derstanding she needed him here tonight, just as she'd needed him after the snake attack. For a man who proclaimed himself antisocial, he tapped into her needs well.

Her needs.

Darcy swallowed.

She glanced at Bo Rokowsky strumming his guitar. She couldn''t help but wonder why she wasn''t in the least attracted to Bo. His dark-haired perfection drew women. His sense of humor held them. He never lacked for anything to say. Problem was that Bo, a man her own age, suddenly seemed too immature.

Yeah. Thanks bunches, Dr. Maxwell Keagan. "You're doing a great job keeping the clueless Romeos and matchmaking Cupids at bay."

"Glad to help." His finger slipped along the silver chain.

The dog tags clinked. Slid. Up. Down. Up again until her breasts beaded in longing for the firmer caress of a warm, broad palm instead of cold metal. "Problem is, you're doing too good a job."

The tags halted. "Huh?"

"Your attentive date touches are making me hot and I'm not referring to sweat."

"Hot?" His hand fisted around her chain.

She needed space. Air would be nice, too. "Way hot. Ducking behind a dune sounds good right now, even though we both know that isn't what we should do." She couldn't keep the hint of question out of her tone.

He exhaled long and slow. Liquid fire raced through her veins, and she was too tipsy and too vulnerable to make a smart decision. This man's experience outstripped her in more than years.

She gripped his hand, slowly untwining it from her chain until they were linked by their fingers and an odd friendship that ruled out impulsive sex. "This has been great fun. But you have some baggage to get over, and I'm not any good at dealing with my own baggage, much less other people's. Please move your hand and let me up."

Without waiting for him to act, she started to rise, a painfully arousing process. Her skin held to his, bonded by the heat and light sheen of sweat, until she was free.

Except not totally. Even as she walked away, she carried the smell of him. Coconut oil, musk—man. Even in her inexperienced state she knew the scent well.

Max Keagan oozed sex.

She needed to control her world, and Max flipped her emotions until she found herself longing to take risks far scarier than plunging into combat. Never again did she want to experience the total loss of emotional control she'd felt during her kidnapping. So she'd always chosen safe relationships that she could manage.

The revelation startled her. No risk. No danger. No chance of being hurt.

She didn't like what that said about her lack of courage. Not at all. Yet, she couldn't stop herself from running tonight.

Darcy spun away to join the safety of her crewdog buds, who never shot sex-laden looks her way, making her question things about herself she wasn't ready to answer.

Max watched the gentle sway of Darcy's hips as she sprinted across the sand to the remains of the supper spread. She snagged a handful of chips and melded into the circle of flyers listening to the guitar-strumming lieutenant.

Where she belonged.

Her edginess crackled through the air. When had he become so in tune to this woman's moods? The notion rocked him. He didn't want this connection with her, but it was there all the same.

Darcy seemed content to let him sit on the outskirts as he preferred. Sure, she'd pushed for him to attend, but respected his boundaries. She might have military regimentation and team play down to an art form, but accepted their differences.

So, what would happen if he gave her that call once he wrapped up unfinished business in Guam? Hell, he'd see her twice a year at best.

He wasn't giving up his career and she wasn't budging on hers, either. And then there was that little matter of emotions. His were limited these days, and he knew better than to expect a miraculous personality conversion once he laid his past to rest. He'd always been a loner, even before Eva. Darcy's emotions flowed in abundance. She would grow dissatisfied with his "grumpiness." Fast.

But, man, it would be one helluva ride in the meantime. If only she wouldn't be hurt in the end.

Max could almost hear Darcy's snort of disdain. *Egotistical as well as antisocial, huh, chump?*

Sit tight. Keep distance and keep quiet.

The bonfire light blotted with a blocking body just before Crusty dropped down beside him, a bag of pretzels clutched in his hand.

"How's it going?" asked one of the least silent people Max had ever met.

"It's all there for you to read in the mandatory reports," Max answered absently, deciding he would keep his answers short and maybe the guy would move on.

He didn't want to discuss work. Not tonight. He wanted to stare at Darcy and tell himself there was a way he could bring her to his bed without bringing chaos to her life.

"You're making progress?"

"What?" Was the guy a mind reader?

"With your *search*," Crusty answered vaguely, his meaning clear all the same.

Oh. Hell. "If you call ruling out negatives progress."

"I do."

Yeah, he wanted this case behind him. Had wanted justice—even revenge—since the day Eva had died. Wanted it for every one of these crewdogs who could be flying over Cantou soon.

Except he'd never before thought about afterward. Darcy made him consider tomorrow when yesterday still consumed him.

Being in Guam again held a time warp quality. It could have been eight years ago when he and Perry had first arrived. Grad students and new CIA recruits before they'd each chosen different paths—Perry opting for low-level agent status to accommodate family life until they'd been paired again for this mission.

"Drinks, gentlemen?"

Max startled back to the present, looking up at the muumuu-clad waitress, their Army CID contact working undercover as an Officers' Club caterer with her *son,* in reality a fellow operative of no relation. Nobody would guess Vinnie with his dreadlocks was actually a civilian employee with Army CID, even given that all branches of the military had a large percentage of civilian employees in counterintelligence.

Lieutenant Colonel Kat Lowry held out the tray. "Mai tai?"

"No, thanks." Max lifted his bottled water. "I'm fine."

"Yes, you are, young man." She passed Crusty a

coconut cup and a grin as she angled closer to Max. "I didn't expect to see you here tonight. Nice reports. You're shaping up, sweetie."

Max pulled a tight smile.

She patted his cheek. Then straightened to flutter a wave. "Be good, boys."

Crusty winked. "Oh, I'm always good."

Lieutenant Colonel Lowry smoothed Crusty's rumpled hair as she sashayed past toward the next customer.

Crusty guzzled from his cup, his gaze fixed on Darcy laughing with Bronco as the big guy whipped out his key chain and flashed a dangling photo. "How many places do you think he can store pictures?"

Max watched Darcy stroke a finger along the plastic-covered photo. Damn it, she should have her own pack of family portraits.

His kid would have been almost two now.

The thought scratched at his insides like the broken shells under his legs. Max tipped back his water and forced himself to swallow.

Crusty dunked a pretzel in his milky drink and popped it in his mouth. "Back when Bronco and I took Wren to the infirmary, Cutter had her hooked up to those antivenom IVs. Cutter and Bronco started passing pictures over her like she wasn't even there." Crusty tossed another soggy pretzel in his mouth. "Bronco, yeah, I expect it from him. But even the prior die-hard bachelor Cutter babbled on about his little girl and new baby boy. Then they passed their stacks to me with big goofy-ass grins on their faces. Know what I mean?"

Max grunted. Perry waggled packs of pictures of his three sons around all the damned time, too. Max always smiled and tried not to think about his own kid who'd never had a chance to pose for photos.

Crusty drained his cup, then tossed it aside. "As if I could tell one wrinkled-faced infant from another. Next thing I knew, I had 'em all mixed up. The two dads looked at me like I'm a moron. Thank God, Wren sorted the stacks and called time-out."

"Sounds like Darcy." Max stared across the small patch of sand at the leggy dynamo flicking coconut milk into Rokowsky's face.

Crusty swiped his arm across his milk mustache. "You gonna call her when all this crap is over with?"

The shells dug deeper right along with thoughts of images never developed. "Damn it, I'm not after your precious copilot who loves babies and puppies."

"Yeah, right. Whatever."

"Doesn't she already have a brother?"

"Yeah, and a whole squadron more of them besides ready to kick your ass if you mess with her."

"This is getting old, Baker." He'd about tapped out his chitchat quota for the day, but knew Baker wouldn't leave him alone without reassurance. Max scrounged up a few more words. "So I've been watching out for her and along the way she became a friend. What's not to like about her?"

"Wren has a way of making friends easily."

Yeah, yeah, Max heard him loud and clear. No need to think he was special, and he had the distinct impression Baker had jabbed on purpose. "Exactly."

Crusty stared ahead, pitching pretzels to scavenger birds. "Those friendships have a way of sneaking up on a guy and becoming a lot more when you least expect it."

Max cut his eyes toward Crusty. Was the guy hung

up on Darcy after all? But Crusty wasn't ogling Darcy. He stared out over the ocean with glazed eyes that seemed to be taking him to another place. Another time.

Hell. Max pitched aside his empty water bottle. Less than a month with Darcy Renshaw trying to socialize him and he was turning into some freaking Sigmund Freud.

Baker swiped a hand over his face, his eyes clear again. "Guys like us don't lead the kind of life that lends itself well to relationships. Too many 'can't tell you where I'm going babe or when I'll be back' moments. Too many secrets."

Memories crashed over him in a tidal wave. He'd lived that nightmare with Eva. She'd wanted them both to get out of the CIA, start a more sedate family life. Had even walked more than once. Not that he blamed her. Even when he was around, he was only half there. Distant on a good day. Distant and hungry for the next mission on a bad day.

He and Eva had weathered more than a few bad days. After his near miss in South America, she'd insisted for a month he back off and take lower risk assignments. Every time she'd traced that scar on his shoulder, she'd cried. If only he'd listened to her and changed the course of their lives, her cover might have never been blown. She might still be alive.

Screw social skills. He didn't want to talk to anyone tonight, anyway. "Get to the point, Baker."

Crusty crumpled the empty pretzel bag. "She's leaving soon. As much as you may think she's clear on the friendship issue, I know her better. As a real friend. And I can tell you, pal, she doesn't look at me the same way she's looking at you."

Max started to disagree, but just his damned luck Darcy chose that second to glance over at him. Her smile faltered. Her fingers crept up to twine around the chain on her dog tags. Did she know how those dog tags of hers turned him on? He wanted to tug her forward with them and…

"Cut her loose." Crusty interrupted Max's thoughts with harsh reality. "Unless you're genuinely interested in her. Then we'll throw you a keg party and give you an honorary call sign. Something like 'Spike' for your hair or 'Fin' for your job. Hell, we can even get you a batch of your own coconut bra pictures." Seriousness stained Crusty's eyes, all the more powerful for its rarity. "Just be careful with her, man. She's got history. She may be friends with the lot of us, but she doesn't let life get deep too often."

Even across the stretch of beach, Max could see those shadows lurking in her eyes. Had they been there from the start and he'd missed them because he didn't know her well enough then? Darcy's file chronicled her kidnapping—with conspicuous holes, thanks to her father's influence, no doubt. She seemed to have moved past it. But of course, what the hell did he know about reading people's emotions?

He could tell what two clicks from Lucy or a head bob from Ethel meant. Darcy, however, constantly defied logic, and he was the poorest candidate on the planet for dealing with things outside his factual realm.

He was right not to call her and to keep his distance from this woman who'd already been hurt enough. "Thanks for the heads-up, Baker, but you're off base. If you're done, I'm going to call it a night."

Max shoved to his feet and stomped the sand from

his skin. Too bad the cutting nicks of shell shards and memories weren't as easily shaken free. And when Darcy left, he would be adding the slice of new regrets to the old.

Darcy shifted restlessly in the base dive shop as she waited for the attendant to bring her diving gear. She hitched a hip against the wooden counter in the sprawling hut and let her gaze wander to the window. The bay beyond the dirty panes tempted her as much as the man who called those waters his second home.

Two days and she would be leaving. Max had invited her to say goodbye to Lucy and Ethel. She understood well enough the goodbye was for him as well.

Her dog tags burned a reminder against her skin of his touch with every gentle sway when she walked. He could have his goodbye, but there wouldn't be any more chitchat with tempting glimpses into the real Max and playful afternoons with Lucy and Ethel.

He'd gone out of his way not to abuse her friendship the past weeks. Which made her want him all the more, damn his honorable soul and cute tush. She wanted a distraction but had found more than she'd bargained for or could handle. In a week she would be sitting in the Squadron Commander's office discussing her chances of shipping out to Cantou.

A rogue thought slapped over her like a wave tearing sand from beneath her feet. She'd accepted the possibility of dying in combat, but she'd never considered how it would affect anyone other than her family.

Max had already lost someone special to him. Was she? Special to him?

Sure it might be overconfident to think she could lure him in for something more. Yet if she did, how would he hold up under the stress of sending her off into danger? Because, damn it, she was not going to spend the rest of her career sitting on the sidelines.

Regret crept up and pricked at her like the sand crab scuttling across the gritty wooden floor to nibble her toes. This really was it for them.

Darcy nudged aside the nipping crab. She intended to make this a farewell to remember, while keeping them busy. No chitchat. Definitely no more touching. Part of her wanted to forgo the farewell altogether, but their time together the past weeks demanded a better end than that.

Darcy waited while the beach bum attendant swiped her credit card and tallied up the day's rental fee for dive gear. The young man with bleached-blond dreadlocks passed her her receipt while his mother scurried behind him in her magenta muumuu.

Flipping the pressure gauge in her hand, Darcy checked the reading for her tank. "Thanks for hooking me up with gear on such short notice."

"No problem, hon." The muumuu mama leaned past her son and over the counter, hoop earrings swaying. "You're not going alone, are you? Vinnie here can dive with you. He's always looking for ways to clock out early, right son?"

The guy was already rubbing zinc oxide on his nose.

"No need." Darcy hefted the gear onto her shoulder. "I'm meeting up with Doc Keagan."

"Good enough, then." The older woman angled back. "Enjoy the day."

"Bummer." Vinnie dropped the tube and whipped

a boxed underwater camera off the display hook. "Here. Take one of these. It's on the house if you show me the pictures later."

"Deal." Darcy hitched her gear over her shoulder.

Jogging down the steps, she tore the wrapper off the camera and arced the garbage into the industrial-size trash bin. Her hand clenched around the camera. Apparently, she would be making her own stack of Kodak memories with Max after all.

A low drone hummed in the distance. Max steered the boat toward the dock. Toward her.

Her stomach pitched just before the scope of her vision broadened and she saw the second figure in the boat. Perry Griffin stood beside his boss. They must have penned the dolphins together.

Damn, but she'd become too well versed in Max's work habits the past weeks. The notion left her feeling more than a little uncomfortable. Of course, he *had* asked her to join him often enough. Some days it seemed the guy wouldn't let her out of his sight.

Max pulled up alongside the dock, eyeing the gear slung over Darcy's shoulder. "I thought we'd planned to meet at the pen."

Was that disappointment she heard in his voice. What a heady notion that he would miss her, too. "I changed my mind. Woman's prerogative and all that."

The boat bobbed and swayed as Perry made his way toward the back to tie off. He nodded to Darcy's gear. "Going somewhere?"

"I was hoping to, if Max is still free." She turned to him. "You said you weren't planning any dives today, just unpenning Lucy and Ethel. The waters are warm enough to dive in swimsuits. So I thought maybe you could show me some of the dive sites if

you haven't timed out on underwater minutes yet…''
She shrugged.

And if he had? There was a limit per day of how
much time a body could stand the depths without suc-
cumbing to decompression sickness, the bends…or
worse, an air bubble in the heart, a concern for her,
as well, if she didn't give herself the proper time between a flight and diving. She prayed her plan for a
no-talk day wouldn't be derailed.

She held her breath and waited.

Max turned to his assistant. "Perry, why don't you
head on in? I'll join you later."

Darcy exhaled her relief.

His assistant tugged a stark white T-shirt over his
head and tucked it into his navy swim trunks, a preppy
antithesis of Max. "Sure, boss. We can review our
data later. I need to give my wife a call, anyway."
He leaped onto the dock and nodded to Darcy. "Take
it easy, Darcy."

Darcy waited until Perry's thudding footsteps along
the planked dock muffled onto the beach before turning to Max. "Wife? I didn't know he was married."

Max draped an arm along the steering wheel, his
chest gleaming deep bronze in the late afternoon sun.
"Going on eight years now."

"Wow. That's incredible. Kids?"

"Three." He frowned.

"Problem?" She edged closer to the dock. "If you
don't want to go, just say so." Just her luck, the quiet
guy would decide he finally wanted a lengthy chat.
She needed her farewell. And she needed it uncom-
plicated.

Darcy dangled the underwater camera between two
fingers. "I want us to say our goodbyes with style.

Make a cool memory to commemorate a special friendship.''

Max's eyes stayed pinned on her for the slap of four waves against he dock before he tipped his head to gesture her into the boat. ''Sounds like a plan.''

Since the man never said much, she took the sign for an all-out invitation and stepped gingerly onto the nose of side of the boat. Max reached to brace her, but she kept her feet sure this time.

Steady.

No wayward body brushes. She had her battle strategy for the day to forget Max Keagan and move on with her life and mission. If only she didn't want to explore his hidden secrets as much as his muscled chest.

A prospect more dangerous to her peace of mind than the next few hours with a half-naked Max.

Robin stood on the sunning deck of the VOQ, time clock punched for the workday, and watched the bay through binoculars from the higher vantage point. Keagan was nowhere in sight.

But out there. Somewhere.

Anticipation fired. Satisfaction wouldn't be far behind. Hours perhaps.

Through the binocular scope, Keagan's dolphins were making their displeasure known from their bay pen. Their clicking and squawks carried on the breeze as they powered through the clear water in frantic circles.

Did they somehow know the time had come for Keagan to die? Perhaps.

Robin lowered the binoculars and returned them to the case. If only Keagan were visible. What a rush to watch him thrash, try to protect his woman, then watch her die before he joined her.

The order had been given.

How the dolphins sensed things went beyond human comprehension. All the more reason they had to be contained at the time of Max's attack. Hell, a couple of highly trained dolphins could provide more protection than a pack of police dogs. Even a lone trained Navy dolphin could protect a ship. Robin shuddered at the memory of a past exercise where one trained dolphin had rather forcefully prevented thirty Navy divers from reaching their intended target.

A dolphin powering by at thirty miles per hour sure disrupted the water and senses.

Definitely better to implement the attack without Lucy and Ethel on hand. Darcy Renshaw had provided the perfect opportunity with her impromptu dive offer.

The attempt to incapacitate the dolphins with tainted fish earlier in the week had only garnered a fifty-percent payoff. Apparently, Ethel had been on a diet.

Thank God Max hadn't located the tap before an alternative plan could be implemented. The guy was so damned close. Keagan's swim pattern now ran directly over the tap, even without a helpful nudge to place him in the position to justify eliminating the diver.

Too damned competent for his own good. Not that it would help today with a force of armed attackers against two tourist divers.

Robin dropped into a white deck lounger and readied to watch the sun set on Max Keagan and Darcy Renshaw's last day in Guam.

Chapter 9

Max stared out over the nose of the boat at the submerged plane wreckage he planned to explore with Darcy. Hell, he hadn't played tourist in...well, never. His and Eva's dives had always been work and training related. But Darcy would enjoy it, and he would enjoy watching Darcy enjoy herself.

His other plan to hang out on a sandbar had been stalled by her tight-lipped attitude. He'd wanted to talk, odd for him no doubt, but Crusty was right. Darcy needed closure for the time they'd spent together. He needed closure.

No luck.

The woman was surprisingly reticent today. He could pry information out from the steeliest sources, but couldn't bring himself to push her. She'd given him space. He'd do the same for her.

Heaven knew she deserved something more from him. Of course she would never know that he'd watched over her. She would likely deck him if she knew his real mission.

If ever a woman balked at being protected, it was Darcy. Not that she would ever know about his job. Or about the real Max.

But she could, a voice taunted. A dumb-ass voice that would lead him into a hellish repeat of the past. Better to exhaust their bodies with exercise. He needed to burn off restless energy, anyway.

Max cut the engine. "You ready, mermaid?"

"Mermaid?" Darcy snorted. "Try to be a little more PC, Doc."

"I stand corrected." He waited for her to send back a snappy response, anticipated it.

Darcy smiled and clammed up, her standard mode for the afternoon, then turned her back to him and gathered her dive gear.

What the hell was wrong with her today?

Shrugging off nagging unease, Max slipped into his own gear by instinct, tracking Darcy's every move to ensure she didn't misstep. Her NAVI and PADI diver certifications reassured him somewhat, but he was leaving nothing to chance when it came to this woman's safety.

With precision, she checked her pressure gauge, then slipped on the vest and tank. Weight belt next, she buckled it well clear of her vest so it could be popped off fast for an emergency rise.

Darcy spit in her mask, then swiped her finger around the seal to keep the mask from fogging up. Max grinned at the ritual. Yeah. She knew her stuff. No one had ever been able to explain why the spit-factor worked. It just did. One of life's great mysteries.

Like why opposites attract.

He pitched that thought overboard before it could tempt him.

Darcy strapped on her fins and slipped the regulator in her mouth. One more glance at her pressure gauge and she taste-tested the air.

She shot Max a thumbs-up, sat on the edge of the boat and fell over backward into the water. Following, he let the ocean swallow him with familiarity.

Lukewarm water. Sunshine streaming through. The roaring of the breathing, a Darth Vader, rushing-in-and-out sound.

Floating into sight, Darcy swept her arms by her sides in a siren welcome. Damn but she was gorgeous, a natural beauty that had nothing to do with makeup or artifice. A novelty for a man who lived with deception.

Max let the air out of his BC vest—buoyancy compensator—and began his descent. Sinking along with him, Darcy pinched her nose through the flexible mask to equalize the pressure.

Down.

Down.

Down with Darcy into the clear water toward the blanket of luminescent greens and rainbow streaks of color below, leaving the world above until it was only the two of them.

Maybe he was overcomplicating things. Likely her silence meant she was ready to cut ties. For the best, damn it.

He would just enjoy this afternoon on his turf with Darcy. He'd learned young to make the most of every moment before the next move. Ignore the rest.

Seventy feet down, Darcy slowed. A cautious diver.

Good. Only pros should dive below a hundred feet where nitrogen narcosis, rapture of the deep, kicked in fast. He didn't need a doped-up Darcy on his re- sistance-weak hands.

Darcy paused to stare at yellow coral fingering out of denser pink bunches, giving a wide berth to the red coral that held skin-burning poison in its spines.

Max pointed toward the looming aircraft. Darcy nodded. He clasped her hand and tugged her with him, kicking, propelling them through the maze of corals painting a Technicolor path ahead of them.

Technicolor?

Where the hell had that freaking poetic notion come from? From seeing the same damn stretch of water he'd covered countless times the past week in a new light.

Through Darcy's unjaded perceptions.

The depths became about more than a workplace full of hidden secrets. Her eyes smiled through the mask at a blue starfish. When had he forgotten about blue starfish? Long before Eva.

Darcy swam in the midst of a streaming school of spotted grouper, then alongside with a manta ray until the four-foot batlike creature finally glided away. Doz- ens of times he'd kicked through these same waters right past this same wreckage and never once had he thought to stop and explore. Not until now. With Darcy.

He'd narrowed his focus for so long while Darcy flung open doors, inviting him into her world. And damned if he could stop himself from joining her, even if only for one day.

Darcy sprawled on the sandbar, diving gear on the beach, their boat bobbing in the distance. Max be- side her.

She was in serious trouble.

The late-afternoon sun cooked her as surely as the time with Max had fried her brain. Something had happened between them underwater, some surreal connection. He'd watched her with such intensity, his eyes all but searing her through his mask until she'd felt linked to him.

She'd been attracted to his body, to his intelligence, even to the boy who watched old sitcoms and played with dolphins to combat loneliness.

Today she'd met the real man in his world. All the elements of Max Keagan pulled together into a total package that touched her. Here, alone on their patch of sand away from the mainland, the boundaries stayed down and she couldn't scavenge the will to resurrect them.

She was weary with fighting the pull between them. Maybe the time had come to take an even bigger risk.

Time to talk. Really talk. "How long has it been?"

Max turned his head along the sand toward her. "What?"

Darcy forced herself to ask the question that would hurt both of them but needed to be voiced. "Since you lost her?"

He didn't look away, blue-green eyes deepening to the color of a storm-tossed sea. "Two and a half years."

"Time doesn't always help."

"No, it doesn't." His chest pumped a half pace faster. The ocean crashed up the shoreline, tipping their toes. Waves drowned out the world and eroded the sand beneath them so walls didn't have a chance of being resurrected. "She was pregnant."

Shock stung Darcy like the spines of poisonous red coral. The sun gleamed off Max's bronzed skin, but his body seemed frozen in ice.

Darcy rolled to her side and let her hand fall on his chest. "I'm so sorry."

He didn't move or touch her back, other than the forceful slug of his heart under her hand. "I went a little crazy that first year after Eva and the baby..." He swallowed. "I did some things I'm not proud of before I found focus."

"To lose someone you love is horrible, but to lose your child, the promise of a family at the same time— you had a right to go more than a little crazy." What would it be like to be loved so fully, passionately by this intense man?

Max jerked upright, her hand falling away. "The baby wasn't planned, but I wanted it. Eva hadn't decided whether or not to take on me and my j—" he paused, frowned "—my lifestyle permanently."

His lifestyle? What was wrong with marrying a professor? Eva lost serious points in Darcy's book if the woman hadn't been able to see beyond the beach bum facade to the serious man beneath.

"Hell, maybe she was right." He hooked his elbows on his knees and stared out at the sun sinking into the horizon. "Who knew what kind of father I would have been? Failing at a relationship is one thing. Failing a kid...I had to get it right. A child deserves more than a father who communicates with grunts." Max shot Darcy a wry smile. "Maybe I have more in common with my old man than I thought."

Guilt pinched her over her teasing and she sat up, swinging around onto her knees to face him. "I might razz you about your…short answers, but you pack more into a few words than most people do in a two-hour monologue.''

''That's a nice thought.'' He hooked a finger in her dog tags as if subconsciously drawn to them. ''But you're reading more into me than is there, Darcy.''

''I disagree.'' She clenched her fists to keep from reaching for him. ''I think maybe there's a lot more to you than even you know.''

His knuckles grazed her cheek, dusting sand away. ''The eternal optimist.''

A smile played with his mouth, and in that moment of closeness, she knew. They'd definitely crossed a line. He was going to kiss her. Their problems still lurked between them, but for some reason they'd both decided to forge ahead.

Her stomach clenched. She wasn't going to launch an advance. But she was done retreating.

Max studied the lips he intended to kiss senseless in less than five seconds. ''You're a nice woman, Darcy.''

''Nice?'' Her smile played with those full and tempting lips. ''Sheesh, if you call me cute, too, I'll have to deck you.''

He laughed. And it felt good. Darcy's optimism made him feel good after a helluva long time of feeling so damned bad.

She didn't move toward him, not even a waver. He'd given her plenty of cause to be wary. He'd bruised her pride. But damn it he'd been in hell himself, caught between protecting her from more coincidences while keeping her safe from him. Right now he couldn't think of a single reason why he needed to do the latter anymore.

Droplets of water from her hair rolled down her neck. Lucky water. He leaned to drink the bead from her skin. Perfect. Satisfying yet addictive.

Max glanced up to gauge her reaction for any sign she wanted to deck him after all.

Her smoky eyes stared back, her lips parted, inviting. Damned if he didn't intend to take her up on the invitation.

Max kissed her finally, fully dipping into the warm heat of her mouth and tasting undiluted Darcy. She locked her arms around him, her hands roving along his bare back with frantic urgency. They tumbled to the sand side by side, and he surrendered to the mind-drugging draw of kissing Darcy.

All the enthusiasm she poured into life flowed over him, encompassed him as if he'd plunged back into the water. Like he was deep in the grips of nitrogen narcosis, his mind swirled with the intoxication of having her in his arms.

Sand beneath them, sun over them, wind stirring up the salty sea air, Max palmed her head and her waist, bringing her flush against him. He traced the high-cut hip of her suit. Darcy moaned, arched closer with an encouraging wriggle.

He tucked his hand inside, cupped the silky softness of her taut bottom. Pulled her closer. Closer again. Nowhere near close enough to ease the throbbing ache as he rocked against her hips.

Max tore his mouth from hers. He had to taste more of her. All of her, in case there wasn't another time. He trailed hungry kisses down her neck, lower to the plunging neckline of her suit. Found the generous curve of her breasts.

Found a tight peak straining against Lycra.

He slipped her shoulder strap to the side and eased the creamy mound free. Tan lines. Max groaned, just before he laved that needy peak. Her fingers clutched his hair, tighter, drew him closer, begged for more. And he intended to give her all she could handle. His fingers trailed forward inside her suit, skimming the seam until he reached…

Her. Hot, wet Darcy. And so damned tight.

Her sigh whispered through his hair just as her mile-long leg hooked over his hip, opening her to his touch. She urged his face back up to hers. The woman certainly knew her mind, and he wasn't arguing in the least since they wanted the same thing.

Her total and complete release.

He stroked, teased…coaxed her closer. Her gasps filled his mouth. Faster. Filled him as he wanted to fill her but couldn't afford to lose that much control even as her breathy moan signaled her own spiraling loss of control. He could give her this much, damn it.

Wanted to see her unravel.

Would see her unravel soon—

Darcy arched against him, her nails jabbing into his back with a half-second warning before her moan split the air. Again, she bowed against him. Her leg locked tighter. Intense. Complete.

Incredible.

She sagged in his arms, her leg around him slackening, her heated huffs of breath blowing over his chest. "Oh…my…gosh. I think I've forgotten how to breathe."

Max let a chuckle rumble free. He should have

known sex with Darcy would be fun as well as intense.

"More," she demanded.

He wanted to comply, but how much farther could it go, anyway, out in the open on a sandbar?

Hell. He knew exactly how far he wanted it to go, out in the open. Darcy soaking up the sun and radiating it right back into him. Him inside her.

She wanted it, too. No question. Her breathy moans and needy arch against him plastering damp Lycra to his chest answered him louder than any words.

The man he'd been two and a half years ago might have taken her up on the offer. But she deserved a better man than that. Now wasn't the time or place for more.

Her hand snaked to the waist of his dive shorts. "Come on, Max. Your turn."

He covered her hand with his. "Later."

"Now." She skimmed her hand lower until her hand found him.

Now sounded good. But not safe.

Her hand curved.

Damn it. "Not now, Darcy." He vise-gripped her wrist. "Later, when you're thinking more clearly. When we're back at the island and can talk this through."

She stared at him with stunned eyes. "You really aren't going to finish?"

His throbbing libido shouted in protest. Never had he been so hot, hard and turned on and they hadn't even had sex.

And they couldn't, not here. Not now, regardless of how much he wanted it. And, man, did he ever want to lose himself in Darcy.

Finally he brushed a thumb over her damp lips. "No."

She bit his thumb.

Not gently. And not sexually. Her eyes sparked as she opened her mouth and swiped his hand away. "I am such an idiot. Silly ol' me thought we had some kind of special connection."

She shoved to her feet and tugged her swimsuit back in place.

Ah, hell, he'd screwed up again. "Darcy, I'm not saying never. I'm just questioning the timing."

"Oh, great. I can hardly think straight and you're able to strategize a schedule for consummation. Nice to know I really sent your hormones into overload, Doc."

He'd hurt her pride. Again. But if he took her here, now when she didn't have a clue who he was…

No. She deserved better.

Darcy yanked her dive vest up from the sand. "I'm so sorry for what you've been through, Max, but I can't let you play mind games with me. I am fed up with people telling me what's right and *wrong* for me. God, I wish you would quit being so freaking protective." She spun on him, blazing anger and jabbing a finger his way. "And don't even toss the birth control protection excuse at me. Because it's not like you plan to follow through even if we swam straight back to a quick-mart."

Indignation radiated from her. Sparked through her. She was so damned hot. And gorgeous. And actually making some sense.

"Besides, I have a Norplant. Are you clean, of diseases, I mean?"

Following her conversational twists was damn well giving him whiplash. "Yeah, but—"

"Me, too. Obviously." She jammed her arms through the vest one at a time. "Yeah, yeah, I know. You're wondering what the hell a virgin needs with implanted birth control. Apparently, I don't need it today."

"Hold on. Let's just—"

"I got it for combat." She plowed over his words as if he hadn't spoken. "I'm hoping like hell I never get shot down, but just in case, I thought I should protect myself." She paused to shoot him a toxic glare. "All of which I would have told you if you hadn't needed to retreat after today's 'interlude' as fast as humanly possible."

Her warrior spirit radiated. Damn, she was magnificent when pissed, and he wanted to kiss her pliant again. But his lack of control had already caused enough damage for one day. He deserved her rant. And more.

Darcy whipped her weight belt off the sand and began securing it around her waist. "Not all captors are sticklers about following the Geneva Convention on treatment of prisoners. It won't protect me from diseases, but at least I won't risk ending up pregnant."

Whoa. What the hell was going on? He struggled to follow the conversation shifting faster than riptides.

Max sorted through her words while she jerked on the rest of her gear with angry hands. She'd never shared her kidnapping experience with him, but he heard the reverberating implications all the same.

He tried to focus on the word *virgin*. She hadn't been raped during the kidnapping. He hadn't wanted to consider that might be one of the holes in her file, but knew too well what those kinds of bastards could and would do even to a thirteen-year-old.

A thirteen-year-old who would have known the possibility existed for every torturous day of captivity. The fear had no doubt left its mark on her.

Max reached for her, needed to hold her and protect her from a helluva lot more than he'd ever dreamed. A dolphin clicked in the background. Not one of his so he ignored it along with reasonable thoughts. "Darcy, okay, you're right. Let's talk now."

She slapped his hands away. "I'm through *talking* to you, Max Keagan. I'm through letting you flip my world. I want my life under control again."

Slipping on her mask, she backed into the lapping tide. His emotions churned like the water kicking up behind her as she charged into the ocean, disappearing into a wave back toward their bobbing boat. He yanked his gear from the sand. She did not need to be out there alone for even a minute. With no dive partner underwater....

Underwater.

The wreckage.

With a buried cable alongside.

The search pattern unfolded in his mind. Clarified...

Why the hell hadn't he considered it before? Just because conventional technology indicated the tap would be on the cable didn't mean it had to be so. What if there was a pulse-detecting instrument close by?

Concealed. Very possibly inside the wreckage where they'd been circling, stirring God only knew what kinds of warnings. Hell.

Max shrugged into the rest of his gear. Double time.

Checked his knife strapped to his thigh. His feet pounded sand as he tightened, cinched, ran, fins last, then plunged into the surf.

He had to haul Darcy safely back to base pronto so he could start a comprehensive search. He would call Crusty to check on her. Max spotted Darcy, a dolphin fin circling ahead. Faster. Alarms jangled in his head.

The clear lagoon waters showed more than the outline of a downed plane and Darcy dipping below the surface. Dark figures, four at least, worked their way toward her. Some might have thought it nothing. Deep in his CIA seasoned gut, Max knew better.

Just like before.

A woman had been targeted because of him.

And this time he would die before letting history repeat itself.

Darcy plunged underwater, welcoming the roar of her breathing from the oxygen tank. She'd wanted a memorable farewell with Max Keagan.

She'd succeeded in spades.

Kicking her feet, she propelled herself deeper, farther away from him, her body still tingling with the lingering aftereffects of his touch. Her life had been so focused just a few short weeks ago. She'd known what she wanted. While she'd been frustrated by the obstacles and delays, she had no doubt that she could succeed in achieving her goals eventually. Never had she let anything stand in her way, not even her indomitable father.

For the first time in her life she was torn with indecision. And all because of one little kiss. Okay, and one really hot, long and insides-searing release.

Damn, but she was confused. She wanted the underwater Max back. She wanted Max. Period.

But she wanted her plane and her independence and some closure to her past. And, God, yes, she was scared spitless of a real relationship. Max might keep his distance with loner solitude, but she found hers through superficial, pal-style friendships.

Being with Max was never simple or superficial. The past hour on the sandbar proved that. His rejection, even a temporary one, hurt. Too much.

She propelled herself forward, drawn almost against her will toward the submerged Vietnam War era bomber. Barnacles encrusted rusting metal. Faded paint depicting a busty woman in a red bathing suit glimmered dimly along the side, rows of brown bombs painted to signify missions flown. Twenty-two before the plane went down. Had the crew perished with the plane?

Rainbow-colored fish streaked through the gaping cockpit window. Darcy startled back. Arms swirling beside her, she stared at the hulking metal, caught in a timeless bond with those who had gone before her.

Those who would go after.

And in that moment she was a part of something bigger than just herself. How odd to feel so very small and yet suddenly so much older at the same time. Her world focused in a flash of time that had nothing to do with proving herself to crewdogs or to her father, and everything to do with living up to the legacy of a group of leather-clad aviators who had taken hits to their craft over a foreign ocean, far away from loved ones.

For loved ones.

In that mystic swirl of water, Darcy Renshaw felt

the determination, the drive, the strength of will that powered countless men and women to give all for others.

And she'd been focused only on herself. Her professional mission. Her personal needs.

How had she strayed so far off course in every aspect of her life? Selfishly, she'd focused only on her need to fight in Cantou, not what the Air Force needed from her.

Even worse, on the beach she'd thought only of her own disappointment, never once considering where Max might be coming from, given what he'd shared about his past.

How damned ironic that in growing up a person realized how very far she still had left to go.

Rushing water swirled, caressing her skin. She needed to wake up. Diving alone wasn't safe and who knew how far behind her Max would be.

A dolphin circled in front of her...Darcy squinted, searched the features. Then reminded herself Max's dolphins were penned, although this one looked a bit like Lucy.

The dolphin swam closer, closer still until she bumped Darcy with her snout.

Ouch. Apparently subtle wasn't this one's strong suit either.

Darcy slowed, stopped. *You want to play?*

The dolphin moved closer, nudged again.

Not right now, if you don't mind. I'm busy running from getting my heart tromped.

The sleek body shoved. Propelled Darcy forward. *Ouch!*

Her side tingled from the powerful push. Unease bubbled through her with as much force as the rushing current around her. The dolphin looked insistent. Even pissed.

Unease trickled down her spine. There were few reports of dolphin attacks, but the mammals possessed the strength and speed to disable her in half a heartbeat.

A diver eased into view in the distance. Thank God. Max would know what to do.

The figure eased closer, clearer. Darker.

No wild dive shorts screamed colors through the crystalline waters. Just an ominous black wet suit. The figure charged forward. Spear in hand leading the way. Followed by another diver. And another.

Unease roared into full-blown panic, certainty—vulnerability. Without her plane. Or even her 9mm.

She was under attack.

Chapter 10

Fear twisted in Darcy's gut, constricting her breathing faster than the dolphin swimming away. But she wouldn't let panic conquer her. Forcing steady drags of air into her lungs, she backstroked behind the wing of the submerged plane. She needed time to strategize.

What the hell was going on? And why?

Wasted thoughts at the moment. She had to concentrate on survival. Questions could come later. And, damn it, she would have a later.

She slid her hand to her thigh, freed her knife, a knife only meant for cutting away seaweed. It was better than nothing.

Blinking inside her mask, she studied the distant cluster of swimmers, at least a couple of hundred yards away. And closing. Two spears glistened, sparked rainbow refractions in mocking arch.

Her mind raced with options unfolding like an in-flight emergency checklist. Could she make it back to shore? To the boat? Or maybe she should continue to hide in the plane wreckage and defend herself until Max arrived.

Even then, her odds sucked.

She considered luring the divers away from Max. For all of three roaring breaths.

Max would find her. No way would he quit searching until he located her, landing unaware into God only knew what.

Warning him would increase their odds. She had to race for the shore and alert Max. Likely he was already on his way. Close. She hoped.

Darcy palmed the knife and kicked. Hard. Sweeping around the other side of the plane and searching the water for signs of Max. At least the clear Guam waters had allowed her the advance warning of seeing the attackers from a distance.

A small advantage, but she'd take it.

Darcy's arms strained. Her breathing labored. She sucked in air from her tank. The underwater beauty she'd so enjoyed earlier dulled to monochromatic grays streaking past. Not nearly fast enough.

Why the hell did this have to happen underwater? She could kick the crap out of two guys on land. Or one underwater. But even with Max's help, these two-to-one underwater odds chilled her. If she could just make it to shore, that would level the playing field.

Her legs pumped harder past a reef of poisonous red coral.

God, she hoped when she hauled onto the sandbar those four divers would laugh and apologize for scaring the hell out of her when they were only hunting.

Instinct told her otherwise, and trusting instincts was critical to flyers who planned to stay alive in combat.

Darcy risked a glance behind her. The gap narrowed as the swimmers streamed over the downed bomber. No more than a hundred yards between her and the four looming bodies and two spears. Did they plan to kill her outright? Or take her, as she'd been taken before.

Panic bubbled up her throat. Darcy propelled by the coral reef. Around.

A figure exploded into view. She clutched her knife. Ready. Her vision cleared.

Max.

Relief punched through her until she couldn't breathe. Had her tank gone dry? Air rushed in. Darcy gestured behind her, searching for ways to make him unders—

He nodded. Knife in hand. He already knew. The clear water must have alerted him as it had her.

A school of fish scattered.

Darcy stiffened. Readied. Blood in the water would draw sharks, but a more imminent threat waited around the reef.

A figure circled into sight, spear aimed straight for Darcy. Eyes behind the mask glinted with pure evil.

No question of his intent now.

Max detonated into action. Yanked the spear, levering the diver forward. Max locked a bulging arm around the attacker's neck. His knife arced down, cut the attacker's air hose with a swift skill and unsettling efficiency that startled her. Reassured her.

One down in only seconds. Hope buoyed Darcy.

A body slammed into her, jerked her arm. Adrenaline surged through her veins, pulsed in her ears. She curled her knees and kicked forward. Thrust. Hard. Slammed the looming diver into the toxic spines of the red coral. The diver twitched, fell away.

Darcy thrashed left, then right, searching for the other two in the distance. She steadied her breathing, strategizing her next move. Another figure slid into view.

Damn it, how many did they have? Already her legs quivered from the exertion combined with their earlier dive. No question, Max's skills in the water outstripped hers. If only she could hold up her own end. She needed to give him an edge.

A hand banded round her arm. Memories of the past blurred with the present, of another hand years ago clamping on her arm at a luau, dragging her away from the crowd.

No!

She powered an elbow back into the attacker's neck. Bought a moment's freedom while Max maneuvered out of reach of a spear and knife.

She sucked in more air. Gritting her teeth for a battle she feared she couldn't win.

And then it came to her. The only plan with a chance of succeeding. She'd just been too trapped in the past to recognize it.

Only minutes earlier she'd vowed that she'd learned, that she would see the big picture in relationships and service. No longer would she seek glory at the expense of what others needed from her.

She hated vulnerability. Hated giving in. But if she continued with her current mode of attack, they could both die.

God help her, she would have to surrender.

* * *

What the hell was Darcy doing? Max swung clear of an arcing knife while Darcy sank.

She descended. Deeper.

Another ten feet and she'd be below the hundred-foot point, in danger of nitrogen narcosis. If she succumbed, she'd be all but helpless.

She had to know that.

She was leading them deeper to disorient their attackers, as well. The consummate warrior and wingman, she knew how to relinquish ego for the good of mission survival. Giving Max an advantage because she trusted he could combat the increased pressure. And he could.

He dodged the next swing of the spear by going deeper. Deeper still. With any luck, the divers would peel away and give up.

Or not. Three bodies powered after them.

Max fought the narcotic effects of the depth. Years of training and experience shifted into overdrive. Lethargy pumped through his veins with a tempting drunken draw, like a six-pack buzz just waiting to grip him. If he let it.

With seasoned practice, he shook it off. Unlike two of their attackers. Already their motions slowed. Turned sluggish.

Victory teased.

The other diver swam straight for Darcy. So damned close. Only a few yards separated them. The attacker caught her flailing arm. Darcy kicked. Struggled. Wasn't any match, not now with the intoxicating effects threatening.

Rage roared in Max's ears, obliterating the rush of air pumping from his tank. He reached…

The attacker's arm cut through the water. The large

blade of a hunting knife gleamed in the glistening depths. The jagged edge raced down toward Darcy. Sliced across her arm. Severed her regulator hose. Bubbles spewed behind her into the blooming red of blood staining the water.

Hell, no!

Resolve iced away the haze. Keeping blood out of the water was no longer a concern, now that Darcy's already leeched all around them.

Max plunged his knife into the attacker's chest. Hefted. Flung him off Darcy.

Her arms slowed until they stopped moving altogether. She stared back with dazed eyes, eyes that slid closed.

Hang on, Darcy. Hang on. From his tank he yanked free the octopus attachment for a second diver and shoved the extra mouthpiece between her lips. *Breathe. Breathe, damn it.*

Crimson blood diffused into a pink haze around them like one he'd seen before. Max shoved those thoughts away before they stole reason faster than a lack of oxygen.

He needed her conscious and breathing before he started the rise. She had to exhale the expanding air in her lungs during a rapid rise.

Time was running out before their attackers might recoup—

Her lids flickered. Foggy, but awake. Not even a second to waste on relief.

He pointed up and locked her slick, too-damned-cold body to his. He had to get her into the boat and the hell away before the other two goons shook off the lethargy.

Rapid rise.

Max secured his hold around her waist. She flung her limp arms over his shoulders in a weak attempt. He unsnapped her weight belt, then his. Infused air into his BC vest. They shot up.

She slumped in his arms. Dead weight.

Exhale, damn it. He tapped her stomach, a light punch to push the air out and combat an insidious threat as deadly as the men lurking beneath them.

The faster the rise the faster the air expanded in the lungs, minimizing time to accommodate. Increasing the risk of exploding the lungs. Instinct screamed to inhale and exhale in a normal rhythm. But one breath of air could be exhaled for an entire rise.

Instinct had to be shut down, the brain assuming control like with a dolphin's controlled breathing. Years of diving had taught him until he rarely thought about it anymore.

But Darcy would be fighting it. And if the air continued to expand without release... Instant death.

Max kicked, rose, rapping Darcy's stomach. The underwater Technicolor that had so mesmerized him during his earlier dive now flashed by in an ominous kaleidoscope.

Brighter. Brighter still as the surface neared.

Kick. Tap. Try to remember how to pray.

The boat hull loomed in sight. Darcy hung in his arms. So close he could swear he heard her heartbeat thudding in his ears with his own.

Max burst through the surface. The fading sunlight blazed in his eyes, across Darcy's face as her lashes slid closed again inside her mask.

He clutched her to him and hauled her unconscious body toward the boat with one-armed strokes. Each slice through the water reinforced his vow. Rules and fair play no longer applied. He would do whatever it took to keep her alive. And if he lost her trust, her respect...her...in the process, it would hurt like hell, but so be it.

At least she wouldn't end up dead.

She hurt too much to be dead.

Everywhere.

Darcy hadn't ached this much since a case of the bends from a rapid decompression during pilot training. She kept her eyes sealed shut and willed away the pain stabbing every joint in her body. Memories painted themselves on the backs of her eyelids. Of the day with Max. Intense pleasure on the beach. Betrayal at his rejection. Horror in the water.

Max!

Her eyes snapped open. Dimmed lights shadowed the stark military hospital room. A bleached sheet and blanket draped over her body as white as the bandage on her arm, as sterile as the antiseptic air stinging her lungs.

Visions flashed of the knife arcing through the water. Down. Her arm throbbed. The rest blurred. Somehow she'd gotten to the surface. *Max.*

She searched the room—the rigid hardwood chair, the gleaming sink, rolling tray with flowers. Her gaze finally landed on the broad-shouldered man standing at the window with his back to her. So familiar. So dear. Her breath hitched in her achy chest. At her slight gasp, the shoulders straightened, turned slowly.

It *was* him. "Hi, Dad."

General Hank Renshaw strode across the room in three long strides. Six feet two inches of lanky uni-

formed paternal concern closed in on Darcy with suf-
focating speed.

"Darcy, baby, you scared the living spit out of me,
unconscious all night like that." He started to reach,
then stopped. His arms hovered in midair, wide in
wingspan like the bombers he'd once flown. "Are you
okay? I don't want to jostle you. I'm going to get that
doctor back in here. Where the hell is he, anyway?"

He pivoted toward the phone as if already prepared
to unleash the full power of the rows of ribbons across
his chest and three stars decorating each shoulder all
over the unsuspecting hospital staff.

"Stop! I'm fine." Darcy took his hand and
squeezed, then shoved herself upright. She fought the
dizziness that would send him into ordering a battalion
of physicians to poke and prod her. "Max. My diving
partner. Where is he?"

Darcy's throat closed on the rest of the words.

Her father's face hardened.

A trembling started in her arms. She forced herself
to swallow. "Damn it, Dad, tell—"

"He's outside the door talking to the security police
standing guard."

Darcy sagged back against her pillows. Screw holding her emotions in check. She'd survived a hideous
day, and her father would just have to take a chill pill.

Then the rest of her father's words trickled through
her relief. SPs standing guard? Her mind swirled with
too many questions.

She started with the most important one. "But he's
totally okay? Max?"

Her father nodded.

The rest could wait. She would ask about the SPs

as soon as she wiped the worried frown off her father's face.

Darcy pushed herself the rest of the way upright and held out her arms. "Come here, old man. I could use a hug."

His arms opened wide as they'd done when he'd found her on top of the cliff twelve years ago. Just as he'd done then, he gathered her close and held on a little too hard as she inhaled the familiar scent of starch and Old Spice. The past hours waiting for her to wake must have been hell on his aging warrior heart.

"I'm okay, Daddy." Darcy reassured herself as much as him. Willed the echoes of the past to dim. A damned near impossible task right now with her emotions already raw.

The day resembled too closely the horror of captivity in a jungle bunker, alone except for the drip of water and the *crack, crack, crack* as the guard outside ate sunflower seeds, pitching hulls into her sweltering cubicle.

Every sunflower seed she crunched open as an adult affirmed her freedom. Her strength over the memories. "It's not twelve years ago. Everything's all right."

"I know, baby."

She fought the irreverent urge to laugh over the "baby" comment, even welcomed the distraction. At least her crew wasn't around to hear. Darcy pulled back, shoving the past aside. "How did you get here so fast?"

He sank into a chair beside her bed. "Caught a hop from Korea the minute I heard."

She jammed a hand through her tousled hair. "I can't believe my crew ratted me out." Irritation stung like the pull of stitches in her arm. "Damn it, I bet it was Bronco, that overprotective lug. I'm going to stuff his lunch full—"

"No one from your crew called me."

And from the stern gleam in his eyes she suspected Bronco and Crusty would pay later.

"Then who?"

"Max Keagan."

"Max?" Betrayal swamped her with a power that made his rejection on the beach pale. He knew how she felt about her father's influence encroaching into her world. Why would he have done that? "So you've met him."

Her father nodded, strands of silver glinting through the brown. Most of those whitening strands had sprouted because of her.

"We've…talked."

Uh-oh. "Could you, uh, ask him to step in please?"

She needed to see Max, reassure herself he was alive. Then she would face the fury and hurt crowding her brain.

"I already planned to." All fatherly concern slid away, the General back. "Given what happened out there today, there are a few things you need to know."

Her father jerked open the door and called into the corridor, "Keagan, could you step in here? It's time for that talk."

She tensed. All the memories of their encounter on the beach and their fight afterward marched over her. What would they say to each other once her father left?

Max stepped into the open doorway. Backlit, he filled the frame with his broad shoulders and magnetism. Darcy's mouth dried. Man, she could use that cup of crushed ice perched on the sink corner right about now.

Then Max stepped into the light.

Her tongue turned to pure cotton.

He stood in the harsh glow of the fluorescent hospital lights, familiar and so very different at the same time. She recognized the outward man in his Tevas, flowered dive shorts and raspberry-red T-shirt. Hacked-off sleeves showcased his diver-down tattoo with that hint of a scar tracing from his shoulder.

The set of his face, the glint in his eyes, however, was completely new. All the events of the past weeks gelled together…his undeclared Glock, his odd dive pattern, why his dolphins still hadn't been released even with so many trips out…

Why they'd been attacked.

Darcy reevaluated that new glint in this man she suddenly realized she didn't know at all. The mindset, however, she recognized well since she'd seen it stamped on so many before him—her father, her crew, every one of those countless faces populating her world since childhood.

She'd wanted Max because he represented something so very different from her father, her co-workers and yes, even herself—government protectors by training, trade and blood.

Looking into his eyes, she knew. He wasn't so different at all.

Max Keagan was one of them.

Chapter 11

Max schooled his features to stay blank, tough as hell to do even after eight years of CIA undercover work. Darcy's look of comprehension—disillusionment—stabbed clean through him.

She was a smart woman. No doubt, she'd put enough pieces together to realize he wasn't simply Dr. Max Keagan. Now necessity, not to mention safety, dictated she learn the rest.

Or at least enough to keep her safe.

He stepped farther into the room, resisting the urge to wince at the ache to his joints from the rapid rise. He'd suffered worse. Luckily the fight had ended quickly. Too much dive time would have added a trip to the decompression chamber.

One small thing to be grateful for in a helluva day.

Okay, two things. Seeing Darcy awake and ready to spit nails shot a bolt of relief through him that threatened to down him faster than their underwater attackers.

The General's eyes landed square on him. Quietly measuring. The old guy still hadn't decided what to think of him. He'd expressed gratitude for the phone call.

Protectiveness had come later, seconds after his military transport plane landed. Why the hell was his daughter tangled up in some covert flight with dolphins, for God's sake?

What the hell was she doing with Max?

He hadn't missed the General's assessing frown. No doubt Darcy's dad hoped the flowered dive shorts were only a part of the cover.

Sorry, old guy. Can't help ya there.

Daniel Baker followed into the room, sweeping around to the side to lounge against the wall and finish off a candy bar. His third since they'd staked out Darcy's door two hours ago.

Darcy's gaze flickered from Max over to Crusty. Shock rippled from her for a split second before her face blanked. Yeah, damned smart woman. Keep quiet until her suspicions were confirmed. She looked away and concentrated on raising the head of her bed.

When she looked back, her composure was solidly in place. "Apparently there's something more going on here than I thought."

Too composed. Max studied the bandage on her arm and reminded himself of his vow to do anything to keep her safe. Her ego would heal a lot faster than another stab from their attackers.

The General stood sentinel by his daughter's bed. "Keagan is a CIA Officer."

The bald statement hung in the air like a toxic cloud.

Max waited for the fallout. Silence echoed, cut only by the rattle of passing carts and the hum from the nurses' station.

Finally a smile tugged at the corner of Darcy's full lips but never made it to her eyes. "That's one damn good cover act you've got going there, Doc.

Accepting the jab as the least he deserved, Max strode deeper into the room. He took up residence by the window so he could monitor the parking lot while talking. "My superiors have sent the okay to tell you some of the background, given what happened. But even with your level of military clearance, understand we can't tell you everything."

Her lips pinched. "Of course I understand. It's my job to understand."

Max winced. Score two for Renshaw. "I'm here to locate enemy surveillance equipment in the harbor."

That much he could tell her since a Navy dive team had already isolated the tap deep in the wreckage. He'd alerted them to the coordinates the minute he'd loaded Darcy into the ambulance. Covert was no longer an option.

Walking away from that ambulance and leaving her in the care of Doc Clark was the hardest damned thing he'd ever done. But finding answers and finishing the investigation offered the best way of keeping her safe.

She'd been attacked because of him. He would never forget that. He was through discounting coincidences. Someone had targeted her because she'd been close to him. He knew it. Accepted it. And wouldn't rest until the bastard responsible was in a cold grave.

A very cold, very deep grave.

While the General explained in more detail, Max let himself study Darcy, reassure himself. Force his heartbeat to stop slugging against his chest for the first time since the divers had advanced toward her.

She was alive, needing only a few stitches in her arm and another night of observation in the base hospital. The day hadn't ended with more blood on his soul.

Her blood.

He damned well intended to keep her alive until he could get her off the island. Security police stood watch outside her door. DeMassi lurked the halls. Kat Lowry and her crew were monitoring every call going in and out of the base.

Max scoured the events of the past weeks for ways he could have done anything differently. The way he saw it, the downslide had started the minute he'd laid eyes on her. The attraction had crackled so visibly any fool could have noticed. And those working the other side weren't fools.

He forced his attention back on General Renshaw's words detailing Daniel Baker's Air Force involvement.

Darcy frowned. "Crusty, too?"

The pilot pitched his candy wrapper in the trash. "Why is everyone always so surprised to find out I have a few connections? Man, sure could give a guy a complex. Yeah, I'm what I guess you could call a consultant on this one. I'm not an OSI Officer, but I run dark-ops testing programs with the OSI, mostly with surveillance equipment. Which made me a logical go-to guy to act as the Air Force liaison on diver dude's mission."

Darcy's gaze gravitated to Max's tattoo. A fire raced below the surface at her fascination with the marking. Did she burn to touch it as much as he burned to be touched by her?

Baker cleared his throat.

Darcy's eyes snapped up, only a hint of pink on her pale face. "Why are you telling me this much now, Crusty?"

"Because we have our man. Thanks to Keagan's direction and coordinates, we've secured the surveillance leak. Once Keagan reached his boat, he deployed forces to track your attackers. They located a body. The security police are running ID checks and have another person in custody now."

"Who?" she pushed.

"Vinnie, the dive shop guy, helped out with O'Club catering. He was found diving in the area."

"But why would he... Oh."

"Yes, that wasn't his real job," Crusty confirmed. "He's a civilian employee working in Army CID— apparently also a mole in military intelligence."

"Civilian?"

"Don't forget nearly half the military counterintelligence workers are civilians—Government Service employees. Our Vinnie is a GS 9."

Max watched her absorb the information of Vinnie's government service status. His arrest. Would she buy the story? Sure the guy had been picked up, but Max wasn't so certain the CID civilian employee was guilty of anything more than a bad hair day. Something didn't sit right, and Vinnie was sure as hell denying involvement.

But Max didn't intend to fire up Darcy with his doubts.

Her eyes lit with battlefield anticipation. "So when do I start looking at mug shots to ID the others?"

The General's hand clamped around the bedrail as if to bar her escape. "You don't."

She sat straighter. "Pardon me?"

"You don't," her father clipped orders. "Keagan here can do that. You're going home."

Darcy's rigid spine kept her upright without any help from the mechanical bed, even while tucked into a standard-issue thermal blanket. A twinge of guilt stabbed Max over calling her father.

He sure as hell understood her struggle to step out of her dad's overlarge shadow. Max scratched his forearm, still burning from just the caress of Darcy's eyes. He'd marked himself with tattoos more than once to claim his life as his own and rile his old man.

Personally, he didn't care anymore or let others' opinions shape his decisions. Running life solo worked better in his job as he'd learned well with Eva. He'd found his place in the world outside his father's influence. He hoped Darcy could find the same.

He expected she would. The General might be overbearing, but Max doubted the old guy had ever leaped from behind corners to knock her on her butt. *Reflexes boy. Don't ever let the enemy catch you unaware.*

Max dumped thoughts of his father out of his head. Must just be seeing Darcy and her dad together that was screwing with his mind.

She pulled herself into a stance that couldn't be mistaken as anything other than military attention. "With all due respect, *sir,* unless I miss my guess, this one's outside your scope of command. There's a bigger picture here and if there's something I can con-

tribute, then by God, I'm not budging off this island.''
She met her father's gaze dead-on. "Sir.''

The two wills, father and daughter, battled so
strongly Max wasn't sure who would win. He had to
tip the odds for the General, no matter what Darcy
wanted, no matter that it chewed his conscience.

Max stepped forward. "Damn it, Darcy, that bigger
picture is about your flying world, too. Leaks like this
can affect every flight plan for the Cantou conflict
coming out of planners on this island.''

He pulled out the stops and voiced what needed to
be said to make her leave. "You wanted to be a part
of the war effort. Well you were a part by getting me
here whether you knew it or not. Time to see the big
picture then and now. You're a military pilot. You
look out for your wingmen and do what's best for
your country. And right now, your country needs you
to get the hell off this island. You're hampering my
investigation.''

Darcy's lips may have stayed closed, but her eyes
shouted across the room. *You bastard.*

The General turned, gratitude stamped on his
craggy face. Apparently, flowered dive shorts no
longer mattered. "Thank you, Keagan. Well put.''

Max stayed as silent as Darcy. Who would have
thought he'd ever side with the starched shirts he'd so
long disavowed? But weighing the options for keeping
Darcy safe, Max accepted he would have to stand in
the old man's shoes.

For a guy more accustomed to Teva sandals, those
polished leathers made for a damned tight fit.

Darcy yanked herself from nightmares full of blood
and sea snakes. She refused to allow herself to scream.

She gasped in drags of antiseptic air, grappling for the chain on the hospital light. Her hand finally swacked it, grabbed, jerked. Light illuminated the room. And the man sitting in the corner chair.

It was *him.*

One leg hooked over the arm of the chair, Max watched her through narrowed eyes. His revelations from earlier rolled over her. The damned irony of it that she'd been a part of the war effort all along.

Not that it made her feel any better at the moment. Just hollow. Tired.

Darcy forked a hand through her tangled mess of hair. She didn't even bother asking how he'd wrangled past the guards. Apparently, this man made his own rules, which didn't include respecting her wishes.

The two-faced rat bastard had used her confidences about her father against her. She wanted Max out of her room, before she did something ridiculous like ask him to hold her until the nightmares faded. ''Visiting hours are over.''

He didn't budge, just continued to pin her with those sea-green eyes shifting with more depths than even she'd imagined. She'd only just begun to figure the guy out, and now he'd changed the picture all over again.

Max folded his hands over his stomach, looking so much like the man who'd waited in her room after the snake attack a few short weeks ago. But that man had been an illusion.

''Well, Max?''

''I thought you might need me after what happened, in case it stirred up bad memories from the past.''

Of the tree snake?

Then she realized he meant the kidnapping twelve

years ago. The past. Of course he knew everything about her from his CIA briefings. Betrayal blazed over her with a fresh vengeance. She'd never stood a chance against him, not when he knew all her secrets, every button to push to wrap her mind so totally around wanting him.

She accepted a certain loss of privacy that came with signing away her life to the military and all the necessary security clearances that entailed. But right now she wasn't feeling reasonable. She felt damned naked and exposed to a man who'd kept everything about himself hidden.

Darcy lashed out with the first line of defense that came to mind. "I *needed* you on the beach yesterday, but you didn't seem to care much about that then, secret-agent man."

He swung his leg from the side of the chair, both elbows on his knees. "You have good reason to be pissed at me."

Damn him and his sympathetic eyes.

"Doesn't take a Scooby Doo sleuth to figure that one out, *Doc*."

Irritation chased across his face. "I had a job to do. I couldn't tell you top-secret, classified business that falls under a need-to-know-only status. I thought you understood that."

She frowned. "I do."

"Then what's the problem here?"

"Problem? If anyone knows about duty and service to country first, you're looking at her. Problem? You're the problem."

"O-kay. Then you're still upset over the beach?"

Hell yes, she was, but she didn't intend to let him know. Especially not now. "Actually, I'm over that.

After all…'' She pinned him with her best Alicia the Icicle imitation. ''You're the one who didn't get to finish.''

Max's brows shot toward his spiky hairline. Good. He deserved a few surprises, the dirtbag.

His brows lowered slowly, assessingly. He studied her through narrowed eyes as if deciphering one of Lucy's or Ethel's clicks. ''Then why are you pissed at me?''

Uh-oh. She should have admitted to the secret-agent-man excuse, an easy out to get him off her back. Instead, she would have to fess up to the truth. ''You called my father.''

Max's jaw thrust. ''Excuse me for thinking your life seemed more important than your pride.''

''Pride?'' Indignation and more than a little pain chased away all traces of exhaustion. ''You think this is about *pride?* It's about being treated with respect. If Crusty were the one lying in this bed, would you have called his mommy to come look out for him?''

He shoved to his feet. ''That's a crock.''

Shock shut her mouth. For two seconds. ''Run that by me again?''

''You heard me.'' He advanced one stalking step at a time, flowered swim trunks riding low on his hips, T-shirt stretched across broad shoulders that had saved her just twenty-four hours before. ''I'm tired of apologizing for keeping you alive the past three weeks. Tired of apologizing for making sure you're safe now.''

He stopped beside her bed, hands planted on the silver rails as he leaned closer. ''Most of all, I'm tired of trying to keep my mind on the job while keeping my hands off you out of some damned misplaced sense of honor.''

He wanted her. Still. For real. No cover act.

And in that burst of realization she acknowledged her secret fear—that he'd been pretending the attraction and she'd been too naive to know. That he hadn't *wanted* to finish.

Hadn't wanted *her*.

Forget backing down. He desired her and she reveled in the power.

She met him nose to nose, this stranger who evoked a now-familiar heat within her. ''Nobody asked you to be honorable.''

A flame lit his eyes a split second before his mouth met hers. Or did hers meet his? She didn't know and didn't care.

She just wanted closer. Deeper. *More.*

Her lips parted under his and he took her mouth. Took her senses. Took her ability to do more than hang on to his neck and kiss him back, explore the taste and warmth of Max, the part of him she knew well.

His hand reached to drop the metal rail, his body following as he sat on the edge of the hospital bed. He cradled her gently, slowed their kiss, savoring, so different but no less enticing than their devouring frenzy on the beach. Their hands explored each other with tender reverence, stealing reassurance that they'd made it through the day alive.

He lowered her back onto the pillow. Not that she put up much resistance, or let go. She wanted to hold on to this moment, to the remnants of familiarity between them. She'd barely let herself dream there could be something more. And it seemed so damned unfair she couldn't have it all.

Max brushed her lips once, twice, again before he rested his forehead on hers. ''What the hell am I going to do with you?''

Familiarity faded, painful reality threatening to intrude. Her hand cradled his bristly cheek. ''You don't get it, do you?''

''Apparently not, Darcy.''

She held back the words for a second longer, held him. For one more selfish minute she wanted to pretend he was just Max Keagan, marine biologist with an attitude.

Her own James Dean rebel with a Ph.D.

Instead…she didn't know what or who he was, and as much as his kiss rocked her, his words chilled her.

''You're not going to *do* anything to me.'' She'd had enough of people controlling her life. She was willing to relinquish control when necessary in the professional world, but she couldn't settle for less than a partnership on her personal turf. ''I understand why you hid your mission. There's nothing to forgive there. But the way you used what I told you against me… That hurts.''

He stroked back her hair with tender, lover hands. ''I'm so damned sorry. But do you know what it did to me seeing you bleeding in the water and your eyes fogging over?'' he paused, his chest pumping with each ragged breath. ''I'd make the same call all over again to keep you safe.''

She swayed forward. God help her, she was weakening, her body wanting to believe the promise in his seductive touch, the pain in his eyes, and just ignore the harsh vow in his words.

The callused pad of his thumb rasped along her jaw, down her neck before his fingers slid into her hair to cradle her head. "You don't think I wish we could back up and be friends again? I don't want us to leave things this way any more than you do." He cursed softly. "There has to be a better way to say goodbye."

Goodbye? Darcy shook off the sensual daze threatening to drain her will faster than rapture of the deep. He wanted her to see the big picture? Fine. They needed to both be professionals and get over their hormones.

Apparently, Max didn't know her very well, either, if he thought she would simply pack up and head home. She swallowed back the surge of longing still shimmering through her. The time had come to take a stand. "Who said anything about goodbye? I'm not going anywhere, *friend.*"

"I swear, she's getting on that plane if I have to carry her there myself," Max groused to Crusty, and paced a bare spot in the industrial carpet of the base security police office.

He'd spent the past two hours watching Darcy scan images on the security police computer screens in hopes of identifying their attackers while DeMassi, Lowry and Perry compiled intel in the next room. He'd looked at the same pictures without any luck, and Vinnie still wasn't changing his story.

Crusty tipped back in the office chair, digging through a bag of mooched sunflower seeds. "Pitch her on the plane? That I've gotta see. The whole John Wayne woman-over-the-shoulder routine will definitely go over big with Wren."

"I don't care, as long as she's off the island." He

watched her frown as she studied another photo. Only thirty-six hours after their ordeal and already Darcy's flight-suit-clad body hummed with restless energy. Vitality. No lingering effects slowing this woman.

Her finger crooked in her dog tag chain, sawing back and forth. What he wouldn't give to hook his finger in that chain and draw her closer.

Maybe they should talk afterward, when she was safe at home in Charleston and he'd put the whole investigation to rest. If only that nagging voice in his head didn't keep insisting he was screwing up by not settling things between them now.

Friend.

He rued the day he'd used that word with her. She was killing him with friendship, treating him like one of her crewdog buds, taunting him with how very much was lacking and how much more they'd had before.

Crusty creaked back in his chair. ''Why not let her spend a few days looking through mug shots until she returns to flying status? She might actually come up with something.''

Max grunted.

''Too bad you were so hell-bent on the he-man 'little woman go home' tactics.'' Baker rattled the bag of seeds, digging for another handful. ''If you'd just let her do her part, this could have been so much more pleasant. She can't leave until she's cleared by the flight surgeon, anyway. She has her old man watching over her 24/7 like a rotweiller.''

Max ignored the pinch of guilt. He'd done the right thing to keep Darcy safe. The general had a grade-A warrior spirit, the kind that would teach his daughter real survival skills and keep her alive. General Renshaw's mindset seemed to go beyond just bloodying a kid's nose with kung fu crap to teach him that surfing was for bums.

Of course, Max had made sure his old man met the mat before heading out to catch the next wave.

Damn. He didn't need the past crowding his brain. A waste of brain cells and energy, anyway.

Max scooped the sunflower seeds from Crusty's hands and started pitching them into his mouth. He crunched and paced. "It's not Vinnie."

"I know."

He almost hated having his gut instinct confirmed. "I've already sent in my recommendation we dismantle the tap. Screw the whole disinformation idea. This is bigger than that. Someone's playing us."

"And that someone's getting reckless."

Max dropped into the vacant office chair across from Crusty. "All the more reason to play it cool. Make like we're content until we have control of the situation." He worked the chair in a lazy half spin from side to side, the spartan government chair squeaking. "The last thing I want is whoever the hell's behind this getting fired up."

"Okay, run with that thought. Let's bounce some ideas back and forth." Crusty waggled his hands. "Brainstorm with me, partner."

Partner? Max paused midcreak.

Brainstorming? Him? What the hell was that all about? More of Darcy's socialization plan. Max stared at her across the rows of steel desks. Intent and focused, she cocked her head to the side to study one photo closer, then waved for the next picture.

She hadn't spared a glance his way, other than another one of her overbright "buddy" smiles when he and Crusty had stepped into the office. She'd nodded politely, of course, then looked away.

Hell. He'd botched things with her on so many levels with no hope in sight for fixing it. He could talk and jam back sunflower seeds until the end of time and he would never have the "socialization" skills to do things any differently.

God, but she was incredible. Max could almost see the stars that would one day gleam on her shoulders. And damned if he wasn't proud of her.

Not that he would let it stop him from seeing her off the island. Rule players like Darcy didn't stand a chance against boundary pushers like himself. It was only a matter of time before he would be standing on the runway watching her takeoff.

Max pitched the sunflower seeds to Crusty. "Time for more of your brainstorming."

His need for solitude didn't mean a thing next to his determination to keep Darcy safe.

Robin fed coins into the sandwich machine in the security police break room, selected tuna salad and snatched the cardboard meal from the slot with impatient hands.

No more time left.

Everything was crumbling.

So much for the promise of caviar and champagne. A lifetime of tuna salad mocked from cellophane.

The final payment wouldn't be wired for a cushy retirement, since the tap had been shut down. The underwater attack had been a complete failure.

Robin dropped into a steel-backed chair and ripped the wrapper off. Only two options remained.

Run. Take the money already stockpiled in the

Swiss bank account and begin a comfortable, if not luxurious retirement. Enjoy the satisfaction of having beaten the system, even though Max would be living out his life when Eva's had been taken from her.

Or...

Robin tore a corner off the sandwich and chewed. End it all in a go-for-broke operation that inflicted the most pain on Max before finishing him off.

Enough of playing the supporting role to Batman, being shuffled aside, handling food, running errands while the big guy ran the show. The moment had come to command the lead for one last kick-ass, explosive, season finale where Batman and his leading lady took their final bows.

Chapter 12

Darcy stared out her C-17 windscreen at the clear morning sky. She'd just completed a flawless takeoff for their return flight to the States. God, it seemed years since Bronco had promised her the cool training experience.

In reality, it was only four weeks ago.

Now she had an expanse of crystalline blue and clouds ahead, her craft humming under her guiding hand. Where was the rush? The excitement she'd expected?

She'd left it behind on Guam with a certain beach hunk turned government agent.

Darcy flipped on autopilot and sagged back in her seat. She hated the way she'd ended things with Max. Sure, anger still zipped through her over how he'd called her dad. And she suspected her father and Max had something to do with the speedy departure orders from Guam just after the general left.

But the danger had passed, they all insisted.

Yeah, right. Max had hustled her off Guam so fast her wheels had probably left skid marks on the runway. Damn both of the overprotective louts, two of a kind, in spite of their radically different wardrobes.

Darcy forced her mind back on her job, monitoring the fuel gauges and assessing the plane's center of gravity as burning fuel shifted weight distribution. The crew compartment droned from engines and the occasional radio call from Crusty in the aircraft commander's left seat position. Bronco sprawled behind him in the instructor's seat reading a book.

She should be reveling in the flight. She lived to fly. Always had, except for that brief time after her kidnapping when she'd resented everything military.

Now all she could think about was what she should have said to Max. Everything she'd wanted him to say to her first.

Instead, they'd both said a whole lot of nothing and a chance had been lost. She couldn't envision what sort of meeting they might have back in the States. But she also couldn't imagine never seeing him again.

Never.

Just the word caused an ache that constricted her chest. She could almost hear Alicia snorting over her shoulder. *So call the guy.* What's the worst he could do?

Break her heart.

And there it was. She was scared to try with Max because defeat would be devastating. The ache in the pit of her stomach swelled.

Crusty thrust a bag of nacho chips her way. "Want some?"

He rattled the bag. The king of moochers sharing?

Darcy searched the label for some kind of gag reading or passed-expiration date.

"No, thanks." She shook her head and transferred her attention back to the control panel.

If he dared crack a PMS joke, she'd off-load him out the back into the Pacific. He and Bronco both stayed diplomatically silent, shooting her sympathetic looks instead.

Worse somehow than being razzed.

Think about work, not about Max and when she might see him again. If she would ever see him. Where she would find the courage.

Ugh! She hated cowardice more than bugs. Darcy flipped through her logbook and updated the fuel reading. She needed to concentrate. No small task in a plane with the capacity to carry 180,000 pounds of gas to balance.

She studied her instruments again, cross-referencing with her notations. Something didn't add up... "Crusty, the center of gravity's moving aft." Not unheard of even though the body tanks of fuel *should* feed evenly. But worth watching. "I'm going to shift three thousand pounds of fuel forward into the midbody to equalize."

"Roger, co," Crusty answered.

Darcy keyed in the computerized shift...and over the space of twenty minutes, watched the same damned thing happen again. She tallied up the math. Twice. Only two hours into the flight and they were already four thousand pounds of gas light. Rechecking her math wasn't going to change the numbers. And those numbers kept shifting at an increasing rate too damned coincidental in a month full of "bad luck" hammering her way.

She'd wanted a second chance to talk to Max in Guam, but sure as hell not this way. If her suspicions were correct, they needed to haul ass back to the island—if they didn't end up ditching in the ocean first. Unease trickled down her spine.

What if the target of Max's investigation had given her a parting gift?

Willing training to override emotions, Darcy keyed up her mike. "Crew, I think we have a fuel leak."

Max stood at the end of the dock that thrust out into the dolphin sea pen. One at a time he flicked fish toward Lucy and Ethel bobbing below with open mouths. Since the incident with Lucy's food poisoning, he'd kept closer watch over what the dolphins ate.

Another couple of days and they would both be released into the wild, due to government cutbacks in funding. He was slated to take the place of a retiring trainer working with the marine mammal program and SEALs at Coronado. A kick-ass assignment that would route him around the world.

After he put the bastard responsible for attacking Darcy into that very dark, very cold grave.

Max flung another fish by rote. At least he had Darcy off the island. Now he didn't have to be cautious for her sake. Finally he could do his job, no holds barred.

His world was so damned silent. The dock so damned empty.

Reaching into the bucket, he pitched handfuls of herring and squid farther into the water. Lucy arched over and away with a splash. Ethel stayed behind. Bobbing. Silently.

Max crouched down and stroked her rostrum. "Hey, girl."

He didn't need to say more. Words weren't needed here. Wise eyes stared back, radiating sympathy.

He understood well that humans only communicated with dolphins when dolphins chose. An irony that was lost on many frustrated trainers—the difference between bribing a few repetitive jumps and developing a working relationship. Odd, but he'd never really thought about it before.

Before Darcy made him stretch the boundaries of his world.

Yeah, he felt the sympathy. Too bad Ethel didn't have any more answers than he did.

A low drone echoed in the distance. Built. Swelled into a siren whine.

Max looked over his shoulder. Foreboding knotted in his gut. "What the—"

The alert siren pulsed. Again and again. *From the base.*

Foreboding fisted into certainty. Max shot to his feet, pounded down the dock and through the gate. Raced for his jeep and launched inside. Cranking the engine, he reminded himself that Darcy was somewhere over the Pacific in her airplane. He'd watched her take off, damn it, to be sure.

But the siren was too coincidental in an op where coincidence had bitten him on the butt more than once.

Max plowed over the rutted road, calling for updates on his radio, cold hard anger growing with each pulse of the siren. Each pulse slamming his temple.

Credentials bought access for whatever the hell he

wanted on this island. He didn't hesitate to use them now to purchase the information and entry he needed.

Emergency C-17 landing. Fuel leak on board, followed by a fire on the runway. Crew taken to the hospital for observation.

Observation. Max kept his breathing steady, palm trees whizzing past as he drove. At least if Darcy *had* been on the plane, she was alive.

Max followed directions to the reception area outside the flight surgeon's office. And found...

Instincts were a pain in the ass and dead-on.

Max stalked into the clinic waiting room. Darcy and her crew sprawled throughout the grouping of stark government-issue office furniture as they filled out seventy-two-hour histories for the accident review board. Tag was nowhere in sight, probably already giving lab samples and receiving an exam. Crusty leaned with his back against the wall, loose, relaxed, flipping through the stack of papers.

Too much so.

Max knew the attitude well—studied disconnection from the event until it could be analyzed from a safer, less emotional distance.

Bronco sat at the table, scrawling on a clipboard, face set, fist resting beside the papers. A fist clenched around a key chain Max knew held a mother/daughter photo.

Bronco glanced up. "Hey, Doc. You must have twisted some heavy duty arms to get in here."

Max shrugged—a damned good cover for working the Darcy-induced kink out of his neck. "What are a few rules here or there anyhow?"

A half smile pulled at Bronco's mouth. He jerked a thumb toward the window where Darcy stood with her back to him. Her fingers parted the blinds to expose the smoke rising in a cloud over the base.

"Wren deserves major kudos. Her quick thinking and air sense saved our asses today. If we'd been farther out over the Pacific…" Bronco's knuckles whitened around the key chain.

Max answered with a tight nod. Anger and something else he didn't want to think about at the moment twisted inside him. He'd worked a helluva lot of ops over the years, had almost bitten it more than once. But he'd kept himself detached from it all, like Crusty over there.

For a damned good reason, especially since Eva.

Detachment gave objectivity. And right now he was feeling anything but objective as he looked at this crew he'd come to know and admire over the past weeks.

At this woman he'd come to know, still didn't understand but had to touch.

Max strode across the room and took her by the shoulders. Just stood, absorbed the warmth of her shoulders, vibrant under his hands, as they both stared out the window.

Max's hands curved around her arms. "Are you okay?"

She nodded, still facing away.

"What happened out there?"

"Fuel leak, so we turned back. Plane caught on fire once we opened the wheel well to lower the gear. Air rushed in, feeding the spilled gas and heat," she answered without turning, her overly controlled tones drifting back. "We landed, ran fast, so it wasn't a problem."

His mind filled in the blanks from her understated account too well.

He leaned closer to her ear and lowered his voice. "You aren't hurt and hiding it, are you?" he asked softly, knowing full well she wouldn't admit anything if she thought her crew could overhear. "You're only a few days out of the hospital."

She tensed under his hands. "I'm fine. No need just to take my word for it. Cutter will have to check us all out, anyway. You can relax. Military airplanes catch on fire more often than you would think. Crusty over there's probably got the seventy-two-hour history form memorized. Just a coincidence that it happened now."

"Do you really believe that, Darcy?"

Her shoulders trembled under his grip, and he wanted to get her the hell out of here where he could hold her. Finally she turned to face him. Soot streaked along one tanned cheek.

It had been that close. The bastard responsible was that desperate.

His hold tightened on her shoulders as if he could keep her grounded and safe through his sheer force of will. A temporary measure. Even though he damned well knew this accident was linked to his case, she still faced similar hazards daily—an unsettling notion he hadn't considered before.

He understood the call to service and the risks involved for her. But had never thought beyond the island. Beyond this case.

Now he had to consider more, didn't have a choice anymore around this woman. Even if he said goodbye to her tomorrow or the day after, he would always wonder and worry. And if, God forbid, something happened to her, it would level him.

He wanted the old days back when he could sit against a wall like Crusty and thumb through paperwork until the world returned to order again. Instead he could only think of the woman in front of him and the fact that he'd almost lost her. Could well lose her in ways that had nothing to do with his profession.

He forced his breathing to slow and reminded himself she was alive. Alive and pissed.

Anger radiated from her in waves as dark as the soot smudging her cheek. "They tried to crash my plane, Max. Some son of a bitch screwed with my airplane."

A rage as intense as hers ignited in him. This crew could have died. *Darcy* could have died.

He couldn't change Darcy's occupation. Or what might happen tomorrow. But he could damn well make sure the son of a bitch responsible for that smudge on her face and shadows in her eyes paid.

Darcy hauled her weary body from the front seat of the rental car outside the VOQ. Bronco, Crusty and Tag piled out, as well. Nobody had the energy left for even a good-night, instead heading straight for their rooms.

Scratching a hand along the neck of her flight suit, she made her way down the open walkway and tried not to think about how much she could use a night on the roof deck with Max. Now that life had slowed, the flight rolled through her mind. She'd half expected the crew wouldn't believe her calculations and would razz her about wanting to return to Guam because of

Max. But they hadn't. They'd accepted her call in the air without question.

Accepted her.

Was this something new? Or had she simply missed it before because she couldn't look past the chip on her shoulder larger than her father's stars? Definitely things to consider. Later. Once she shucked her flight suit, showered off the layers of grime and slept for twelve hours. Longer.

Never long enough to forget how good it had felt relaxing back into the comfort of Max's hands on her shoulders. He always knew when she needed him. She—a woman who prided herself on never needing anyone.

And there he was.

She shouldn't be surprised. Max leaned against the wall in the shadows outside her room, thumbing through a copy of the base newspaper while he waited.

She wasn't fooled by his relaxed pose at all.

Muscles rippled with tension along his bared arms. His diver-down tattoo flexed and twitched as if protesting the restraint of Max holding back. Ready to pounce.

He flicked to the next page of the base paper without looking up. "Wanna head up to the deck or go inside?"

"You assume I need you now like after the snake attack and back in the hospital."

He would be right, not that she intended to admit it.

Max closed the paper, folded it in half and tucked it under his arm with precision. "Maybe I need to see you."

Well, hell. The guy sure knew how to sap the air

out of a girl's anger. Darcy jammed her key into the lock. "Okay. You've been a good friend. You've seen me, checked up on me. I'm really fine. Or as fine as can be expected when I've almost died twice in a week."

And she hadn't even flown combat. Talk about a crash course in survival. She swung open her door and strode inside. His determined footsteps tracked her into the darkened room.

Darcy flipped the light switch and pivoted on her boot heel. "Good manners dictate you wait to be invited in."

"Thanks for the tip. I'll take it under advisement."

"The new Max is even grumpier than the other one."

He didn't budge. "So I've been told. Thanks again for the etiquette lesson."

His broad chest offered comfort, calling to her with a power more intense than an embossed invitation. Especially with an empty bed only five feet away.

She needed space. Now. Maybe if she ignored him he would leave.

Darcy plopped down in a chair and started untying her boots. She thumped one, then the other onto the floor, and still Max loomed by the door. Would the guy ever get the message?

Standing, she hooked her hands on her hips. "Leave, please, so I can get some sleep."

He took a lazy step nearer to her. To the bed. "Do you really want me to go?"

"Yes." No.

"All right, then." He absorbed her with the slow ride of his eyes one last time before he turned to grip the knob.

"Max!" Damn. She bit her lip.

He didn't turn back. Just waited.

Damn him again for making her be the one to say it. But he'd been right in the hospital. They couldn't leave it like this.

She let the question fall from her mouth, a question that had tormented her insecurities. "Is that your real name?"

His hand fell away from the door. Slowly he turned, and she was confused all over again. She didn't recognize this man any more than the Max of the weeks prior. The man of the past few days.

She looked closer and found...he was pieces of both.

Could that be wishful thinking? She didn't know or have the energy to wade through it all at the moment. This man stretched her comprehension on a good day.

This had not been a good day.

He stepped forward, closed the space between them and extended his hand. Took hers in warm callused heat that was oh-so familiar. "Hi, I'm Max Keagan, and yeah, that's my real name, although I've answered to others on occasion when the job called for it. I have an undergraduate degree in biology from Stanford. A doctorate in marine biology from the University of San Diego. And somewhere along the way to typing 'the end' on my dissertation, I accepted an intriguing offer to work for the government."

She listened—and heaven help her, even believed— all the while wondering why she couldn't bring herself to pull her hand from his enfolding grasp.

Her toes curled in her socks. "And the part about being a military brat, was that just a cover story? A way to get closer to me so you could—'' she winced on the bitter word ''—'protect' me?''

Max looked into Darcy's eyes and realized his answer could mark a beginning or end. His choice.

He could so easily slide into any number of personas he'd donned over the years and send her running. That would sure as hell simplify things. He'd checked on her. Found her safe. He could walk away as he'd done countless times before.

He could. But he wouldn't. Not now that he knew it wouldn't make any damned difference. This woman had taken up residence in his head and he didn't have a clue how to evict her. Damned well didn't want to.

''Hell, yeah, I wanted to protect you. But the parts about my past, my father,'' he forced himself to say, ''Eva and the baby. All true.''

A sigh shuddered through her. Seeing how much that simple admission mattered to her piled more guilt on top of the old. She deserved better than he could give her, not that he could stomach the thought of anyone else stepping into his place.

She wanted him. He wanted her. And after a week of having almost lost her twice, he couldn't bring himself to turn away again.

Max pulled her closer until she resisted, inches shy of contact, her heat grazing him all the same. ''That wasn't the only truth. I wanted you, Darcy, so damned much it dogged me every minute, all day, every night. But I couldn't take it further, not when I couldn't be honest with you.''

''So you never have sex while undercover?''

God, he loved her spunk. She wouldn't make this easy for him, but who the hell wanted easy, anyway? ''That's not the point.''

She shook her hand free and backed up a step. "Then make your point, friend."

He advanced, invading her space just as she invaded his senses. "Yeah, I resisted for the job, to protect you and for a selfish reason, as well." A truth he'd only just admitted to himself. "I wanted you to be with *me,* not the person you thought I was."

Damn it, look at me, Darcy. See me.

Her hand raised, slowly, almost as if against her will. She touched his arm with just one finger along his tattoo, tracing the inked edges along his bicep. "And now I feel less like I know you than when you stepped into that briefing room a month ago."

Another damned coincidence since he didn't feel like the same man anymore. Darcy had torn down so many walls, demolished defenses.

One elegant finger abandoned the tattoo for the scar disappearing into his sleeve. "Would you have ever told me who *you* are, even after this case?"

Leave it to Darcy to slice straight to the truth. He'd lied to her about so many things, had so many things from his job he could never tell her. He needed to be honest now. "I don't know what I would have done. But I do know you got to me, the way no one else ever has. You still get to me. Realizing something could have happened to you today, earlier this week, is burning at my gut. Yeah, I'm here because I want to protect you. And I'm not going to back off or apologize for that."

He locked his fingers around her wrist, stopped her tantalizing touch while soaking up the feel of her satin skin. "But what I said outside is true, too. I'm also here because I have to hold you."

The defenses fell away from her eyes, leaving

Darcy standing in front of him for the first time since she'd stalked away from him on the beach. "God, Max, you may not talk often, but when you do, you sure know how to level a woman."

Taking her words for consent, he dragged her into his arms as he'd wanted to do since he'd seen her filling out forms at the hospital. Hell, since the first time he'd seen her in that briefing room back in California.

He held her close, probably too tight, and inhaled the scent of her. Soap and baby powder. Darcy and innocence tinged with the harsh scent of smoke making him want to hold her all the tighter.

Her chest rose and fell, faster, heavier, until her breasts brushed him. Tightened. Bringing an answering tightening in him, an arousal she couldn't miss, pressed so closely to him. Her fingers tightened on his shoulders, but she stayed silent.

He understood her hesitation. He'd pushed her away so many times, hurt her pride once too often. She wouldn't ask. Now to lay it all out there and hope she didn't opt for revenge. A risk well worth taking for a chance to be with her.

He didn't know where they were going. Or how the hell they would manage the aftermath. But he was certain of one thing.

No more holding back.

"Darcy," he whispered against her hair.

"Yeah, Max?" She didn't move or even look at him. But she didn't pull away, either.

"I want you. I wish I could find prettier words for you than that, but you already know I'm not the most communicative guy on the planet. You deserve to hear how damned incredible you are. Except the more I talk, the more I'm finding there aren't any words that come close to doing you justice.'' He eased back to stare deep into her eyes and repeated, ''You deserve to know.''

Max cupped her face in his hands, determined to show her a much better way to communicate with their mouths than talking.

Chapter 13

Who needed talk?

Darcy flung her arms around Max's neck and backed toward the bed, her lips parting to accept the warm sweep of his tongue. Answer him with the touch of her own.

Her fingers combed through his spiky hair as she'd longed to do countless times since she'd first eyed the sun-kissed strands. She submerged herself in the sensation of his coarse hair rasping over her sensitized skin. Not because of a need for risks or adventure, but in a heart-twisting hope to connect with Max on a deeper level.

They'd both almost died. The thought tore through her—that they might never have shared this moment. That she could have lost him before she'd ever had the chance to really know him.

She would know him now, if only on this superficial level. A meeting and mating of their bodies to affirm life.

Darcy molded herself closer to the hard wall of his chest and struggled to will away somber thoughts. Some things in life were beyond her control. Finding a way to hold on to the special bond with Max might well be beyond her control. She gripped him tighter, locked him closer, not nearly close enough.

Max buried his face in her hair, his hands low, guiding her hips against his. "I wish I could take you somewhere special, memorable, out under the sun. For weeks, I've wanted to peel that bathing suit off you, make love to you on a sandbar." He stroked the back of one finger down her neck, lower, dipping into the collar of her flight suit and hooking around her chain. "See you wearing nothing but the sun and these."

Her dog tags dangled from the crook of his finger.

Darcy glided her hand along his cheek. "Seems to me we've already had the wide-open-spaces experience, and it didn't end very well for us."

His hand clenched around the chain. "No baggage from that day."

She totally agreed. They'd earned this time together, damn it. She arched up on her toes. "Here is good." Perfect. "Any military brat worth his salt should know it's not where you are but who you're with that counts."

"Touché. And now you're about to be with *me*."

Darcy stared into his eyes, deeper, and saw him because finally he opened himself up enough to let her inside. This man who was too well versed in keeping his identity hidden.

But not now.

He wasn't the moody doctor of the weeks prior or

the driven operative of recent days. But Max, a man who wanted her. No games here. She might not have a clue about what made him tick, but there was no mistaking his desire for her—a heady aphrodisiac.

A thrill of anticipation tripped along her adrenaline-heightened nerves. She waited, wanted…

His lips found the throbbing pulse at the base of her neck. Who'd have thought anyone could have so many nerve endings in one patch of skin? Her head lolled back and she sighed. She inhaled the warm sunshine scent of his hair as Max inched the zipper down on her flight suit, following the revealing path with his mouth.

If only she wasn't so aware of how long it had been since she'd put on that flight suit. How damned unfair that he smelled like coconut oil, sunshine and a hint of musk while she likely reeked of sweat and smoke.

She clasped his hand. ''Max, wait.''

Groaning, he dropped his head to her breasts. ''You're gonna make me be honorable, aren't you?''

''No.'' Definitely not. ''I need to shower first. I know it's probably unromantic of me to want to delay, but man, Max. A girl only has one first time and—''

He hooked an arm behind her knees and swung her up against his chest.

''Max!''

''You want a shower, lady, you're going to have a shower.''

Why hadn't she just suggested they shower together rather than admitting she smelled like a crewdog? Alicia's voice mocked her as they crossed the room.

Way to go, kiddo.

As much as she and Max might be equals in the work world, his experience in the sexual arena left her

in the dust. His past included women who likely wore
lace or silk and not a green flight bag with white athletic socks.

She hated encroaching insecurities, especially when
she prided herself on conquering in any field she
chose. Hang tough and be bold. She wanted this. She
wanted Max.

He turned sideways through the bathroom door. He
set her on her feet in front of the shower stall and
reached to turn on the water.

Darcy looped her finger in the drawstring of his
flowered swim trunks. "Maybe I should get a tropical
shirt so we'll match."

He cupped her face between both broad palms.
"Darcy, there's so much light and life in your eyes,
in you, clothes couldn't compete." His sea-green gaze
devoured every inch of her. "And there's something
so damned sexy about the way you're completely covered in that uniform. Makes me want to…"

He grasped the tab on her zipper and tugged farther.
Slowly. Link by link he pulled until he unveiled the
hem of her black T-shirt and a hint of underwear.

The combination of his words with his stare hotter
than any jet engine swept away insecurities.

Max grinned. "Layers. I like layers. Sometimes the
payoff is all the sweeter when you've had to work for
it."

His hands slid inside, cupped her bottom, his arms
shrugging the flight suit from her shoulders. Darcy
whipped the uniform down and off, kicked it free
while pulling her T-shirt overhead.

Until she stood in a sports bra and high-cut panties.

His low growl of approval caressed her ears,
swirled inside over feminine instincts. His fascination

with her dog tags, the way his eyes had so often lingered on the high-cut hip of her bathing suit, all told her that while he might opt for flamboyance in his own clothing choices, he in no way found hers lacking.

Then with two bold sweeps of his hands, her underwear fluttered to the floor. And she knew by the heat of his gaze as he stared at her wearing nothing but her dog tags, he definitely didn't find her lacking.

Sliding his swim trunks down and off, he backed her into the shower before she caught nearly enough of a glimpse of him. Warm spray sluiced over her, warmer still as the water heated.

Or maybe *they* heated the water. A definite possibility.

Darcy trailed her fingers along hard muscle and Max, down to his hip, discovering another tattoo. Poseidon's trident sliced across a hard hip, launching a tingle up her arm.

She'd spent her life around men, had stumbled into more than a few locker rooms with minimal privacy situations on the road. She might be a virgin, but she wasn't naive about the male physique, and man, oh, man, did this guy have a body to make her go weak-kneed against the wall.

Water rained onto his head, saturated his hair, darkening it. How perfect that he should be surrounded by water. Seeing him through the spray somehow made him seem all the more familiar.

She traced the cut of muscles along his chest, to his stomach, a solid wall of tanned heat. Her hand journeyed lower until she wrapped her fingers around him.

Her back flattened against the shower wall.

Max anchored her to the tiles a second before his

mouth slanted over hers. His body pressed a hot, hard melding of wet skin to skin until she could almost feel the water evaporating off her overheated flesh.

His hand left her. But before she could even groan her protest, he returned with a bar of soap. Anticipation curled through her. She reached for the washrag dangling from the showerhead.

He grabbed her wrist, lowering her arm. "You won't need that. Quit trying to take control of the jet here, Darcy. There are two of us running the show."

His hands and soap glided over her. All of her. He washed her, washed away the horror of the past week, carefully easing his fingers over the puckered pink scar on her arm. He swept away memories and boundaries with his broad but gentle hands until only the two of them stood together in the waterfall spray.

So very bare.

Then his hands slid up her neck into her hair as he worked in shampoo. Bold, callused fingers massaged against her scalp and every nerve with such thorough intensity. His eyes never left her face while he watched her, as if he had to see what he was doing to her.

And, oh, he was doing so very much to her.

He tipped her head back, stroked his hands over her hair, swiping the soap away from her face so she could keep her eyes open, as well. Water cascaded down her, washing away suds and restraints.

"No more," she pleaded, wanting him out of the shower and on dry terrain where she could tumble him into bed, onto his back.

He grinned. "Much more, Darcy."

Max dropped to his knees.

Heat crawled up her face at even the thought of

such intimacy. The whole standing-up-in-a-shower-stall idea was already stretching her limited—hell, nonexistent—experience.

She gripped his shoulders, her nervousness and breath-stealing excitement warring for dominance. "Uh, Max. This might be a little advanced for me just yet. How about we slate this one for maybe, oh, our third time?"

"Darcy?" He brushed his lips across her breasts, drank from her skin.

The sensation made her light-headed. "Yeah, Max?"

"Hush." He drew harder on one taut peak. "Unless you want to tell me exactly how this feels. Then you can be sure I'll listen to every damn word."

His mouth claimed her other breast. She sighed her answer, tracing the tattoo on his arm with trancelike intensity along the red edges of the rectangular flag.

Diver down.

Hot breath blew across her stomach. She shivered with a rush of pleasure. Okay, she could get into this.

He kissed lower. Lower still until bold hands nudged her legs. Parted her. Tasted her.

Her knees refused to support her.

Thank heaven his hands did. Broad palms cupped her hips, lifted and secured her against the shower stall as he spread her farther with his shoulders. Darcy flattened her hand to the wall as sensation washed over her with each glide of his tongue. Her pulse pounded through her veins just as the powerful spray of water throbbed against her body. Need throbbed even lower still.

Built. Swelled. Exploded over her, sending rainbow

shards of light sparking through the water spraying over them.

Delicious shimmers rocked right through, leaving her thighs shaking and her body craving even closer connection. She twisted her fingers in his hair and tugged. "Now, Max, really no more."

He rose through the steam, kissing his way up her body, cupping her breasts to drink the water from each tip before he grazed over her neck. Finally he met her face-to-face.

"Much *more*," he repeated, molding his body to hers, lifting her.

Her feet dangled. She was losing control. And it would be so easy to lose control with Max calling the shots. She trusted him. She wanted him. But some stubborn part of her still yearned to employ a few seductive moves of her own this first time. If only she had the confidence here she had in her plane, where no matter what fate threw her way, instincts ruled.

Instinct. The number-one flyer rule—trust the instincts.

A slow spiral of women's intuition as old as time smoked through her. She draped her arms over his shoulders. Instinct guided her foot up the back of his calf. He groaned.

Satisfaction spurred her. Oh, yeah. Instincts definitely ruled.

She hooked a leg around his hip, bringing them both closer. The heat of him throbbed against the cradle of her stomach, ready. She refused to let fears or insecurities tense her. She wanted this, everything. Now. Instinct would guide her on what to do next.

Darcy shut down her brain, closed her eyes and readied to fly straight into the mist.

Max gritted his teeth, trying like hell not to fly out of control, instead to press gradually, carefully into the satin grip drawing him deeper. Darcy's Norplant allowed him to enter her without anything between them. He could feel every square inch of her. Deeper until he met resistance.

He steadied his breathing. Willed himself to go easy. Take it slow for her. A damned tough proposition with Darcy arching against him with a needy sigh, bringing herself down—

She winced. He tucked her close and stilled, water, steam and silken woman against him, around him while he waited, chest pumping a ragged pace under the strain of holding back. But he would, damn it. For her.

And then she moved.

Man, did she ever move. Darcy hitched her leg higher, rocked against him with a natural rhythmic grace that threatened to send him hurtling over the edge.

Not yet.

He guided her against him, slower. Her other leg swung up and around his waist with the athletic fluidity that marked her every move.

Forget restraint. He secured her against the wall. Damned grateful for the support himself, as he thrust and lost himself in this woman. Knew he didn't ever want to walk away. Swore he would find some way to make this last as long as he could, as if that might somehow lengthen their time together before real life crashed down on them.

His eyes absorbed the vision of Darcy, surrounded by steam and him, water streaking down her face. A face so intense and focused on finding release even while prolonging it.

The need to finish twisted inside him, pounded through him in an urge to finally and completely claim her as his. Her breathing hitched, her full breasts pressing against his chest faster with each deeper breath until—

Her cry cut through him, cut through his restraints. The strength of her release gripped him, sent him hurtling into completion right after her.

Water beaded down her head. Their bodies too close to let even a drop slide between, Max held Darcy backed against the shower wall while aftershocks ripped through them both.

This competent, incredible woman needed him, whether she wanted to admit it or not. She needed *him.* And for the first time in his loner life, Max understood what it meant to need someone, too. Totally.

And what it would mean to lose her.

She'd lost it. Totally lost it.

Darcy curled against Max's side in her bed and wondered where her will to fight had gone. She wanted to hide in this room and make love to Max until they both couldn't walk.

Of course, she wasn't sure she could manage more than a few steps at the moment after her bone-melting release in the shower. Max had carried her back to bed, so she still hadn't tested her legs yet and couldn't see herself rolling out of his arms. Not yet.

Too bad real-world worries and concerns didn't respect closed-door boundaries. She couldn't stop herself from asking, "What was she like?"

"Eva?" His eyes closed, he didn't even pretend to

misunderstand as he stroked roughened fingers along her stomach. "Emotional."

Jealousy sucked. An overachiever all her life, Darcy couldn't swallow down the thought of coming in second. She needed to know the competition, the stakes suddenly too high. "I was looking for a little more from you than that, Max."

The backs of his fingers continued their lazy dance across her waist. "We never could figure out how we ended up together, both so damned different. But we spent so much time together working ops—"

"Working together?"

"She was CIA. I guess I never told you."

Shock pinched right along with the increasing sting of jealousy over a woman who'd shared so much more of Max than she ever would. "Nope, that wouldn't have come up in the past few weeks."

Since she'd barely known him then, either.

"Eva wanted out." Max's low voice rumbled in the cinder-block room. "Even before the baby, she'd been thinking about leaving the Agency."

His muscles contracted across his chest. She rested a palm against them until they relaxed under her touch, then traced up to explore the scar on his shoulder. "How did you feel about that?"

"It was her choice."

"And?" Her finger etched down the white line of scar tissue slashing through his dark tan. A knife wound. No question. How had he gotten that scar? Could he even tell her the circumstances if she asked? Given his job, there were things about his life, pieces of this man she could never know. Another obstacle to consider.

"Eva wanted me to get out, too." He opened his

eyes and turned his head toward her. "I couldn't do it, Darcy. I couldn't buy into a scenario where we both taught Marine Biology 101 for the rest of our lives. I sure as hell tried. How damned ironic I ended up playing the professor to find her killer. Why the hell couldn't I have just made the change when she was alive?"

Her hand curved over his scarred shoulder. "The Dr. Keagan thing is a part of you, but it's not all of you. Not like being an agent is."

"So it would seem."

And how sad that the understanding should have brought them closer but only widened the gap. No way could she envision him following her around from base to base, swapping university appointments. Max wasn't a follow-around kind of guy. And she respected him for it, even as she wished they could both be different.

Max stroked Darcy's damp hair from her face and wondered how this woman had figured out so much about him in such a short time when he and Eva hadn't understood each other after years together.

"I didn't love her enough." Max ran his hands along Darcy's arm, stopped to cup her hip through the sheet. Would he be able to do any better by this woman?

"Maybe she didn't love you enough."

"Run that one by me again?"

Darcy tucked the sheet higher under her arms. "Maybe I don't know what I'm talking about, or maybe I'm just being judgmental because I'm jealous as hell of her right now. But it seems to me you never asked her to change herself to be with you."

Her words rolled over him, seeping deeper. He

would never reconcile not having been able to save Eva. Hell, it had been just a regular swim that day, since she'd already started her paperwork to leave the Agency—a swim that went all to hell after they'd made it through so many ops together unscathed.

No, he would always have to live with her death. But Darcy's words reached him. Yes, he and Eva had both tried like hell to make the relationship work. He may not have loved Eva enough, but he'd done the best he could then by her in life. Maybe with time he could accept that much.

Darcy winced. "Of course, now I'm realizing what a pain in the ass I must have been about my luau socialization invitation."

Max looped her dog tags around his finger and tugged her closer, nose to nose. "There's a big difference between asking a guy to quit the CIA and pushing him to hang out at a party." He loosened his grip, grazing his fingers across her delicate collarbone. "You don't have anything to be jealous of."

Darcy tugged her chain free and sat up. "I wasn't angling for anything with that comment. No need to feel pressured into thinking I expect more from tonight than we had."

"What the hell's that supposed to mean?" He wanted more—and more again, even out of bed when they had their clothes on. He wanted more time with her.

"I understand about adrenaline letdown. We both almost died this week." She wrapped her arms around her knees and pleated the sheet between her fingers. "We're…friends…so the stress is doubled."

Shock sucker punched him. Max sat up and turned

her to face him. "You're kicking me out of your bed."

"I'm telling you that you can leave."

"Maybe I don't want to leave."

"Geez, Max." Her fists punched the mattress, pulling the sheet too damned taut against her breasts. "I'm being straight with you. Don't play mind games with me."

"I'm not the one playing here, Darcy. You're the one who's running scared."

She jabbed a finger in his face. "Don't you ever, ever call me a coward."

"Then why the hell are you so damned scared to have a conversation with me?"

He stared into her unblinking eyes and couldn't stop the replay of those same eyes sliding closed with pleasure as water streaked down her face. Why was he pushing this? He should just flip her on her back and slide into her until they both couldn't think, much less talk.

Darcy looked away. She rolled from the bed and to her feet, taking the sheet with her. She scooped her boots off the floor and dropped them into the closet.

She knelt to tug his T-shirt from under the bed. "We are talking."

No they weren't. He was freaking losing his mind while she played Molly Maid. "We're not talking. You're asking questions. Poking and prodding at my past. You talk and talk but you never share one damned piece of yourself."

Darcy shot to her feet and nailed him with angry eyes. "I told you about my father, and look what you did with that information. You used it against me."

"Okay. I deserve that." He pitched aside the lightweight blanket and sat on the edge of the bed. "But I think I also deserve a little slack because keeping you alive seemed more important at the time."

Her stormy face calmed, his T-shirt dangling from her hands. "What about later? After I learned the facts and wasn't operating in the dark. You could have given me the choice whether to stay or go. Except you didn't trust that I would make the right decision. You didn't trust that I can protect myself."

He grabbed the trailing hem of his T-shirt in her grip and dragged her forward until she stood between his knees. She'd demanded he open up to her and she could damn well reciprocate now that she'd unlocked the floodgates. He wasn't hanging out on top of this wave alone. "Why is being able to protect yourself so important? You still haven't told me."

"You know why." Her gaze never faltered, but her skin chilled against the embrace of his thighs. "You've read my file."

"That's not the same as *you* telling me." His hand grazed up to palm her neck. His thumb stroked her soft cheek. "You'll let me into your body, but you won't let me into your head."

She jerked as if slapped. Darcy hitched the sheet higher as if to shield herself.

Flinging his T-shirt in his lap, she backed away. "You want my guts spilled all over the floor? Fine. I was kidnapped when I was thirteen years old. An extremist terrorist group, who wanted the military base gone from the island, decided to make their statement in a big way."

Her words gathered force, rolling out of her in the hurricane he'd unleashed. "So they snatched me from a luau, right under all those damned flyers' noses.

They took me. They locked me up in an old World War II bunker and kept me there for a week.''

The pain in her voice in spite of her composed face jolted through him with as much power as her words. Hearing, seeing what she'd been through shredded his insides. He'd witnessed scenarios like hers before firsthand while pulling someone out of a hell like the one she described. But this was Darcy.

Damn it, he righted these kinds of wrongs for a living. A totally illogical part of him wanted to have been there for her then. Resolved to be there for her now.

Boundaries be damned. He yanked her back into his arms and dropped her into his lap, her spine as straight and rigid as her unbroken will.

But she didn't pull away.

He stroked his hands up and down her back and let her talk. He'd asked for this, after all, and he would see it through for her.

She clutched that shield of a sheet in a white-knuckled fist. "If I made any noise, they threw bugs and rats in there to keep me company."

Max forced the red haze of fury away as he thought of what hell she must have endured the past weeks with all those "accidents."

He wanted to find the person responsible and kill him. Twice. Except her records indicated they were already dead, taken out during the raid to rescue her. "I'm so sorry, Darcy."

She laughed, a wobbly half effort that brought his arms tighter around her. "So, yeah, I have intimacy issues. I like my personal space. Big flipping deal. It doesn't stop me from getting up in the morning and doing my job. It doesn't stop me from living my life.

And if I'm not living it the way you want me to, then tough. Just who do you think you are making me spill my guts like that?''

The answer burned in his gut, in his brain, words he'd never wanted to say again, much less feel. ''I'm the guy who loves you, damn it.''

Chapter 14

Darcy reeled from Max's words echoing in her head. Her intimacy issues were taking some serious boundary hits tonight.

She should be dancing. He wanted her. Even lo—

Damn. She couldn't even think it. Couldn't breathe as she sat in the circle of his arms. Still, she felt so much for this man. And it scared her. Max was supposed to have been safe, first as the moody professor, even later as the driven operative—both men who wouldn't make demands on her emotions.

The words were right there in her head, waiting to be spoken. Waiting for her to throw away control and give over her life and herself to a chance with this incredible man who mesmerized her even as he confused the hell out of her.

"Max." She pushed the word out. "I—"

He shook his head, cupped a hand behind her neck, urged her forward and just kissed her.

Man, did he have a way of just kissing her.

Her insides melted. She hooked her arms around his neck and lost herself in the moment. Tried to ignore the insistent voice telling her she wasn't being fair. She was using sex to avoid talking. She knew it, but couldn't make herself stop. How strange that Max could voice his feelings while she hid behind desire.

A desire sparking through her with all the heat of an afterburner. Desire and emotions, too, whether she wanted them or not. But what *did* she feel for this wild, unpredictable man who'd so captured her attention, from the minute he'd sauntered into her life?

She didn't want to think. Just wanted to feel. So much easier than sorting through emotions and the risk of opening her heart.

Being vulnerable.

She wanted control back. Somewhere. Somehow. Of something in her life. Instincts. She could trust those.

Go with it.

Darcy surrendered to the moment, the sensual caress of Max's lips on her skin. Hers on his. He whipped the sheet free and pitched it aside. She trailed her fingers down his chest, along his scarred shoulder. Felt his strength. Reveled in rocking his control.

Her hands glided around to his back, his skin so hot under her hands as if he'd soaked up all the sun's rays. That heat seeped right back into her until it pulsed through her veins, chasing away the chill of childhood memories.

And how she welcomed losing herself in Max. She slid from his lap and dropped to her knees.

His hands fell to her shoulders. ''Darcy—''

She took him in her mouth and whatever he'd

started to say choked off in a groan. She let those instincts guide her into new, uncharted territory she very much wanted to explore. She lost herself in the moment, in the unbridled pleasure of giving pleasure until Max gripped her arms and hauled her up.

"Enough," he growled, hooking an arm behind her legs and tossing her on the bed.

Max blanketed her with his body, elbows keeping the bulk of his weight off her, simultaneously sheltering while exciting. She savored the steely strength of him stretched out over her, yet wrestled with the need to flip him on his back. Be the one over him. But as she'd found only moments before, even in taking control she surrendered.

His pleasure was hers.

She couldn't conquer or control. If only she could find an equality, a way to hold on to herself and have him at the same time.

Then Max rolled to his side, pulling her onto hers.

Confusion niggled, threatening to slow her momentum. "Max, help out the rookie here."

"A rookie? Not for long." Max cradled her thigh in a firm but gentle hand and urged her leg over his hip, bringing her closer as side by side they faced each other. No one above or under.

How did this man seem to recognize the wants she hadn't even given voice to? Damn but that scared her.

Excited her.

Her leg locked around him as she guided him into her body. Wanted to let him into her heart. What would it be like to spend years, a lifetime even, being challenged by this man who saw beyond boundaries? Made his own rules, yet respected hers, at least here.

It could be…everything.

Slowly he filled her, stretched her tender body and stared into her eyes while giving her time to adjust. He communicated so much through his eyes. Why hadn't she ever realized that before? He didn't use words. He sensed.

Sensed her fears. Sensed her needs.

Now.

And somehow he heard her. His hand rasped lower to cup her bottom, guiding her forward. Meeting her. Moving inside her, deeper, until she forgot about logic and concerns and just felt. Felt and moved, heat tightening, building low and intense. Enough, and at the same time there could never be enough to make her stop wanting more. More of him.

His hand slid between them, palmed her breast before sliding down, touching, finding, bringing...

Completion.

Max sat with his back against the headboard and watched the glowing numbers on the bedside clock blink away the night—2:00 a.m.

Darcy lay on her stomach sleeping, her face turned away from him as if she wasn't ready to see the morning or him yet.

True enough.

The hurricane shutters might be blocking out parking lot lights, but it couldn't stop morning from arriving, anyway, in another few hours. He knew Darcy well enough to understand she would likely start running. Soon. She would rebuild her boundaries before facing him again. If she came back.

He needed more time and they didn't have any, not with a case to close. But he sure as hell wasn't letting her climb back in another plane until they had the people responsible for her emergency landing in custody.

So he watched the clock and counted down the minutes until he would have to leave her.

Darcy stirred, burying her nose in the pillow before turning to look at him with blurry eyes.

I'm the guy who loves you, damn it.

His words from earlier hovered between them.

Yeah, he'd meant it. He just hadn't meant to say it. Not yet when he wasn't even comfortable with the idea himself. How could he expect her to be? But the words were out there waiting to be dealt with.

He picked a strand of hair from her lips and tucked it behind her ear. "I meant what I said."

A tight smile flickered across her face and he recognized Darcy-the-buddy trying to slide between them and a real discussion.

She slugged his shoulder lightly. "Your delivery could use a little work, then. That was a helluva romantic way to say it."

He gripped her chin in a grasp not as gentle as he'd planned and tipped her face up to his. "That's because love isn't always pretty. It can tear you up inside. I've been there. Done that. Got a few scars to show for the effort. Love is a damned scary proposition, Darcy."

She flipped to her back, her sad eyes staring up at him. "You want me to say it, too."

Did he? Hell, yes. And no. Part of him wanted a safer, easier life for her than whatever he could offer. "I don't think you're ready."

She grazed her fist over his shoulder again, her fingers unfurling to caress him. "I should slug you again for telling me how I feel. Except I'm too tired tonight...and you're right."

Her hand fell away. She sat up, elbows on her knees and shoved her hands through her tousled hair. "I'm such a mess, Max. I do want you. I want more of everything, not just—" she waved a hand over the tangled sheets "—this, but everything. Talking. Not talking. Being together. I want it all with you. But you're right. This is damned scary, and more than anything, I hate being out of control and afraid."

Max resisted the urge to drag her into his arms and insulate her. Letting anyone—him—get close seemed to top her list of fears. He couldn't fight that one for her.

She picked at the lightweight blue cover. "After they found me, I really thought I was handling it all. I mean, damn. It wasn't like anyone had assaulted me. I should be fine, right?"

He stayed diplomatically silent, trailing one finger down her delicate spine. So rigid even now.

"Three months later Alicia chewed out our dad, told him I needed help processing what had happened. She made him drag me to a counselor on base to talk through everything." She smiled over her shoulder. "Nobody says no to Alicia. Not even the General."

"She sounds like her sister." Max tapped her stubborn chin.

"I went for about six months, and it helped. I really thought everything was okay for years. I even stocked up on sunflower seeds in defiance of the terrorist who chowed down on the things while guarding me."

Max worked to hide the protective urge she wouldn't want or welcome. "Sounds to me like you did a damn fine job at coping."

Darcy's smile faded. "Then the world situation started heating up with Afghanistan and Sentavo, now

Cantou. The memories all began crowding back in my brain again. The more my father put the stops on a combat assignment, the worse the helplessness became.''

She shifted over onto Max's lap and straddled his legs. Her palms landed flat against his chest. Intensity hummed from her. ''I want to fly, Max, and I'm not afraid of combat…well, not any more than a normal person should be. I hate it that all this is coming back up to screw with my mind.''

Damn being distant. He hauled her against his chest. ''Have you talked to anyone else about this?''

She tucked her head under his chin, the scent of her shampoo drifting up. ''Not since the counselor. I didn't even tell the civilian investigators most of it. The people responsible died in the raid when I was found. I wasn't ready to think about the snakes, much less talk about them.''

He tried to follow her convoluted retelling without slowing her momentum. ''Snakes?''

''While I was in the bunker, I developed a level of tolerance for the bugs and even the rats after a couple of days, or just hid my fear better. So they pulled out the big guns in the pest department. That's how they punished me for trying to slip secrets to my father during the phone calls.''

He could just see Darcy in battle mode, even at thirteen, staying calm, strategizing when she must have been scared as hell. He stroked his hands up and down her back.

She shuddered. ''They held snakes to my face. Let spiders crawl on me. Honest to God, it was easier to fight off the attackers underwater than to deal with all those bugs these past weeks, and then there was that damned snake in my room.''

His hands slowed along her back. Information shifted in his head like pieces of a puzzle looking for a clean fit. "Darcy, tell me again who knows about the snakes. The cops?''

"No. I didn't even want to say the word *snake*, much less chitchat about them. My dad cleared away any public records and most of the military ones, as well. I worked through it with the counselor and then put it to rest. Or so I thought.''

He took her shoulders and eased back. "Your counselor would have made notes. Right?''

"Sure, sealed, though.''

Ah, hell. Max hefted her off his lap and onto the other side of the bed. He rolled to his feet and scooped up his swim trunks.

"Max? What are you doing?''

He yanked them on while searching for his shirt. "Sealed *military* records. Records that someone with deep military intelligence connections would be able to link into for ways to get to you because of your connection to me. Someone with high-tech surveillance experience to work with the tap.''

Her brow crinkled, her mind racing to catch up. "Military intelligence personnel dealing with surveillance equipment?'' Her eyes widened with dawning horror. She shook her head. "Not Crusty. It isn't him.''

"No. He was on the plane with you yesterday and could have died, too.'' He jammed his arms through his shirt and whipped it over his head. "Not Crusty. Kat.''

"Kat? I'm not following here. I'm still stuck back

on the idea that someone read my sealed records to torment me with my worst fears.''

''The O'Club caterer.''

She wrapped the sheet around herself and stood. ''That sounds like a stretch to me.''

Max grabbed his wallet and keys. ''Lieutenant Colonel Kat Lowry, Army CID, posing as mother to Vinnie the civilian agent.''

''Hell, how many of you are there on the island?''

''More than I wanted.'' Of course having Kat Lowry off the op wouldn't have stopped her. If his suspicions were on target, she'd been at this for years.

Darcy's hands knotted in the sheet as if trying to anchor her to the bed, when she no doubt wanted to leap into the middle of the action.

No, his gut insisted. He burned to tell her to go back to sleep. He would handle everything.

Except if he voiced that gut reaction, she'd clam up. Walk away. And rightly so. He would feel the same. ''We could use your help piecing this together.''

Shock sent her eyes open even wider. He shouldn't be surprised. He'd done little to earn her trust. Even now he fought the urge to recall the words and plop her gorgeous ass onto the first plane off the island.

''I'll get dressed and follow you over soon.''

His hand hesitated on the knob. ''I'll wait for you.''

She waved him away, the sheet still shielding her. ''Get going. There's no time for you to wait. I won't be long. I can use a few minutes to get my head together before talking through all this again.''

Vulnerability flickered in eyes already ringed with dark circles and shadows. He charged back over to the bed, kissing her hard and fast, branding her as his before he left. Darcy needed her space? Fine. He'd give her space. But that didn't mean he was walking away.

Darcy stepped out of the shower for the second time in a few short hours. Not as satisfying a cleansing as the first one, but enlightening. Every drop of water that rolled down her skin reminded her of sharing the same stall with Max. Soaked into her with reminders of how much she wanted him in her life.

She reached to swipe steam off the mirror, her hand slowing. As if guided against its will, her finger traced through the fog until a diver-down symbol appeared.

Her arm dropped. Geez, she was like some schoolkid scribbling "Mrs. Max Keagan" on the back of her notebook.

Whoa! Wait. Where had marriage thoughts come from? She pressed the heels of her hands to her eyes.

I'm the guy who loves you, damn it.

The walls crowded in on her as if she was in that bunker again. She wanted to trust everything would work between them.

Yet emotions were different and far more fragile than the body. A currently tender, well-loved body.

She wanted to trust Max would always be there for her, but she couldn't erase the sense that one day she might be left waiting. Hurting. She knew intellectually her father had found her in record time. She would have sworn she didn't blame him. But had she subconsciously been blaming him all these years?

Irrational. Stupid. And flat-out wrong, except who said emotions were logical? Hers definitely weren't these days.

Intimacy issues.

If she never let anyone get too close, no one could ever let her down. What an unrealistic expectation to set for herself and for any man—perfection with never a misstep. Of course she'd been the one to misstep.

He'd told her he loved her. And she'd hid in that mental bunker like a scared kid rather than take his face in her hands and thank him for the beautiful gift of his heart.

Even if she couldn't pull her own messed-up head and heart together enough to be the woman he deserved, she should have kissed him. At least been brave enough to tell him the truth, that, yeah, she was halfway there to being in love with him, too. She should have given reassurance that with his patience she could kick down her own walls and join him.

After twelve years of closing herself off, maybe it was finally time to let someone inside. Let Max inside.

Starting now.

Darcy slipped on a clean flight suit and laced up her boots. Heading out the door, she prepped her mindset for battle. Losing wasn't an option when the stakes were forever.

Steam radiated up from the parking lot even in the middle of the night. She strode down the open walkway, dim lights tracking her way toward her rental car while stars dotted the sky overhead.

Halogen lamplight silhouetted a man lounging on her trunk, his back stretching a preppy, blue polo shirt.

"Perry?" Darcy called.

Max's assistant straightened and spun to face her. "Hello, Darcy. The boss sent me over to pick you up. He said you didn't need to be driving after all you went through yesterday with the emergency landing and all."

That sounded like Max. She started to argue and assert that she could drive herself.

How ridiculous and recklessly prideful. Why not take the ride? She could use the time to settle her emotions before she faced him again, rather than climb behind the wheel with shaking hands.

One brick at a time. Pull those walls down and quit being so frigging defensive. "Thanks. I appreciate the thoughtfulness."

Night silence echoing, Darcy stepped around to the passenger side and slid into the sedan. The air conditioner blasted her with arctic air. No wonder Perry looked so crisp without even one stray hair mussed in spite of the hundred-plus degrees outside. "You must be eager to get back to your wife and kids. How much longer do you expect to be in Guam?"

Streetlights whipped past the windows, haloing his blond preppy perfection. "Not long at all. We've just about wrapped everything up."

"Good." Which meant Max would be free sooner. Her stomach performed aerial maneuvers.

Perry braked the car to a stop at the sign in spite of the nonexistent traffic, before turning onto a narrow road behind an oversize cinder-block building. "Too bad you can't go diving with Max since you just flew. Wouldn't want to risk an air embolism."

"Huh?" Darcy yanked her attention away from concerns about how she and Max would handle trying to make a relationship work in the real world. "Even once the time restriction wears off, I'm not so sure we'll be wanting to dive together anytime soon."

She stared out the windshield and steadied her breathing by counting fence posts in the distance, a fence with wire mesh tubes strapped to catch tree snakes. Spotlights showcased one long carcass trailing from the end of the tube.

She shuddered.

"That sure was a close call for you and Max, all those divers coming after you." A smile picked at the corner of Perry's mouth. "Good thinking on your part, using that red coral to your advantage."

Red coral? How did he know?

A tingle iced up her spine so cold it canceled out even the a/c blast. Surely she and Max would have recognized Perry as one of the divers attacking them.

Had she or Max told anyone about the red coral?

She couldn't remember for certain. But if she hadn't, Perry could only know by hearing from someone else who'd been there.

The tingle flamed to a burn.

Trust instincts.

Darcy reached for the door handle and eyed the approaching stop sign. She didn't care if it looked silly, her falling out on the sidewalk. Crusty and Perry could tease her later if she was wrong. After the week she'd had, no way was she ignoring her instincts.

Instincts fired to full alert.

Screw waiting for the next stop sign. She yanked the door handle. The door wouldn't move.

Don't panic.

A hand banded on her arm. "Careful, now," Perry crooned. "If you want to stop, just say so."

She balled up her fist. "Okay, I want to stop."

"No problem."

Her eye caught a flash, low, in Perry's hand.

She arced back to punch. Nailed him in the face.

A pinch, then a sting spread through her leg. Confusion swirled. A spider again? She looked down.

A syringe dangled from her thigh, piercing through her flight suit into her skin. An empty syringe. Oh, God.

"You son of a bitch." Darcy knocked it aside, kicked, screamed, prayed like hell someone would hear her before whatever he'd given her…started to…slow her reflexes.

The edges of consciousness sucked inward like in a rapid decompression. Fogginess rolled over her. Consciousness faded with Perry's voice echoing in her dazed mind as he pulled from behind the building and drove through the front gate.

Perry swiped the trail of blood from his nose, his blond hair not so neat anymore. Darcy didn't have time to appreciate the damage she'd done with her right hook as reality drifted with his fading voice.

"Let me tell you about an episode of Batman and Robin where Robin decides it's time for him to run the show."

Chapter 15

Max peered through the window into the security police station interrogation room where Lieutenant Colonel Kat Lowry sat, ramrod straight and not budging on her responses. Her voice echoed through the speaker as she answered routine questions from the steely-haired OSI Special Agent.

Alone in the narrow observation hall, Max processed her answers piping through the speaker. But more important, he studied the Army intel officer's eyes to gauge her reactions. He absorbed her every betraying twitch, already compiling a list of rebuttal questions to pass along to the interrogator.

After a quick briefing from Crusty and Max, the OSI had picked her up hours ago—a cold victory, revealing a traitor. Hell, it all made sense. Her encryption specialty with the tap. Her knowing precisely when Max and Darcy had left to dive. Her ensuring Vinnie was in the wrong place at the wrong time to appear guilty.

How many other minds and lives had she played with? The scope of damage could ripple for years. The Army CID officer perched in the steel-backed chair with a calm no doubt honed from years in the field.

He'd waited for this moment since Eva's death, longed to find a link to the intelligence leak in the South Pacific. Still, the closure didn't settle within him.

Max rested his palms on the ledge and canted closer to the one-way mirror while she answered another round of questions. His gut told him they had the right person. She insisted she didn't need a JAG, but he could sense the edginess in her even through glass.

Yeah, it fit. Almost. He couldn't reconcile the image of this woman wasting time on spiders or tampering with a plane to taunt Darcy.

The tension in Lowry built until Max could almost see it pulsing from her, like the heightened Technicolor world he'd missed underwater for so long. Darcy challenged the hell out of him, bringing all senses alive until the world sharpened.

Focused.

Until he could see Kat Lowry was ready to…

"I want to cut a deal."

Max exhaled the victory.

Her voice remained calm through the speaker. "You can arrest me—just one solitary little leak." She leaned forward, elbows on the table. "Or I can give you at least fifty military and CIA leaks in exchange for immunity."

CIA? Alarms jangled in Max's head.

"Colonel," the interrogator intoned, "I don't have the power to grant that and you know it."

"Find someone who does. You can buy me off with

a deal. Piece of cake. Other countries have been doing it with money for years. And while you're at it, here's a token of good faith, a freebie to give you a sample of what I know. Maybe soften the folks farther up the chain.''

The interrogator folded his arms. ''I'm listening.''

''Max Keagan's assistant.''

Perry? Max searched Lowry's face, deeper, wondering what game she was playing with them this time. Confusion shuffled the new piece of information in his brain seeking a place in the puzzle.

The interrogator shot her a skeptical look.

She waved a hand through the air. ''Your choice whether to believe me or not. Your loss if you choose wrong. He was placing encrypted phone calls to me right up to a few hours before he left San Diego. I'm telling you, he turned and he's out of control. He's got some kind of vendetta against Keagan. A person like that is dangerous. Damned emotional bastard blew this whole operation.''

Max scrubbed a hand across his face to clear away lack of sleep and search for what reason Perry would have to go gunning for him.

Kat Lowry drummed her fingers along the steel-topped table. ''Perry Griffin's been selling information for years. Hell, he's the one who tipped off the other side so I could wrangle myself in on the intel team to control the fallout. He's definitely got an agenda this time, and he won't accept less than the personal satisfaction of watching Keagan suffer.''

His hand falling away from his jaw, Max studied her face and found—determination.

He believed her. He didn't need any more words for confirmation even while all those pieces of information jammed against each other in ragged mismatching order.

Slowly she turned to the one-way mirror. Max felt her eyes smolder through. Connect.

No way could she see him, but her eyes locked dead-on. ''Keagan might want to call and check up on his girlfriend.''

Her implication popped right through the glass and into his brain like a bullet. Pierced him with a grinding certainty.

Snakes. The plane.

Screw wondering why Perry had it in for him. Where the hell was Darcy? She damn well should have arrived by now.

Max reached for the government phone on the wall. Snatched up the receiver. Punched in her room number at the VOQ.

Ring.

Pick up, damn it.

Ring.

Pick up.

Three more rings. He slammed the phone down. Maybe she was on her way.

Except, his gut told him that because of him she was being thrown back into the hell of twelve years ago that she'd only just begun to come to grips with. His heart slugged against his chest in protest.

His feet carried him down the hall to find backup, no more Lone Ranger when Darcy's life was at stake. Max forced himself to think. Think like an investigator. More important, think like the person who would have tortured an innocent woman with horrors from her past just to get to him.

Max focused on climbing inside Perry's twisted mind. He had to figure out where Perry would take

Darcy. Find out—and get there before the sick bastard killed her for a personal revenge Max couldn't begin to understand.

"You're a sick bastard." Darcy pushed the words free.

She stepped out of the car into the isolated tropical clearing, each movement like flying through peanut butter thanks to whatever drugs had lurked in Dr. Demented's syringe.

The door slam echoed in the pre-dawn silence, in her throbbing head. She didn't even want to consider what animal tranquilizers might be pumping through her system.

This sure made for a rotten morning-after in the wake of the best night of her life with Max. She had no intention of dying today, but she couldn't help feeling a twinge of gratitude that she'd had her night with Max. Just in case.

And he loved her.

Slumping against the rental car, she stared up the deserted path to the looming cliff of Lovers' Leap. The whole climb looked so much more ominous in the haze just before the sun would break the horizon. Sweat trickled down the neck of her flight suit in spite of the salty breeze blowing in off the water.

The ocean roared in the distance like the roaring in her ears, almost as if she'd already been submerged underwater. She had no doubt but that Perry planned to drown her, one way or another.

Her chances of winning a fight were minimal with the drug in her system. Would the effects worsen? Should she take her chances now? Or would she rouse with time?

Soon, please.

Two Perrys wavered in front of her.

''You're one tough lady to kill. Puncturing that fuel tank was difficult to arrange and not as creative as I would have liked. But you're really frustrating the hell out of me.''

Good. She intended to continue right on with that mode of attack.

Darcy planted her boots as a twelve-inch lizard scampered by in the negligible light. Odd how the critters bothered her less when put into perspective with the human reptile in front of her. ''I can't walk up there. Not with what you've given me.''

''Yes, you can.'' He tucked his shirt into the waistband of his khaki shorts with meticulous care as he scanned the landscape. ''I was careful with the dosage. I enjoy the planning, the precision of lining up every detail. You can walk.''

She let her legs fold until she sat on the soft pad of grass, too tired to care about lizards. ''I *won't* walk.''

If he had to carry her, his hands would be occupied. She would find a way to stop him if she didn't have to expend all her fading focus on standing.

Perry reached behind into his waistband. His hand whipped back around, her vision wavering in a jerky haze.

The cold barrel of a gun pressed to her temple.

''Walk,'' Perry ordered. ''Or I'll shoot you now. Not creative at all, but in this case, I'll settle. Your choice.''

No choice at all. She braced a hand on the warmed metal of the car, prayed for balance and shoved to her feet. Palm trees swelled around the stretch of dirt trail, animal sounds echoing from their branches. The twining vines and floral island scents that had seemed so lush and beautiful during her walks with Max now suffocated her.

Jamming a hand in the small of her back, Perry propelled her up the winding path. "I'd much prefer to weight you down and toss you into the ocean, then let you die of an air embolism as you rise. That would be so dramatic. Definitely creative. And it would be quite poetic for you to die in Max's world."

Perry swacked aside a branch to clear her path in a perversely gentlemanly manner. "But you're damned spunky. I would have to use too many traceable drugs to subdue you enough to put on a wet suit."

She let him talk and ramble while she searched the dense path for some sign of an early-rising tourist, anyone to help her.

"Plan B will work as well. The mild dose of animal tranquilizers I used on you should pass an autopsy. Max will know I did it, but will never have his proof. He'll have to live with that nagging question in his mind. He'll know that his picking up Kat Lowry alerted me to finish you. Now."

Live. Max would live. Relief soaked through her foggy brain. She pumped air into her lungs as she huffed up the path. At least Max would survive this nightmare. She could hold on to that.

She didn't even want to think about what it would do to him to lose another woman he loved.

Perry jerked her elbow to guide her. "I wanted to kill him, too, but time's running out before they'll be on to me. Given a choice between you and him, I'll pick you and let him tear himself up with guilt in a living hell."

Darcy stumbled, twisted her ankle. Damn. The sting burned. At least the pain lanced through her fog.

She reached for consciousness. Rational thought. Stay alive. Just stay alive.

Lethargy pulled at her limbs and her will. She battled the urge to lie down and surrender to the driving need for sleep.

Darcy forced herself to put one foot in front of the other. Her boots thudded a steady cadence along the moist, black soil. March, soldier. Old ROTC days blended with childhood echoes. Quitters never win and winners never quit.

Her old man's philosophy had its merits.

Blinking away the grit in her eyes, she trudged up the slope. Finally, after twelve years of avoiding this place, she stepped into a clearing atop Lovers' Leap. Fading stars sprinkled the sky, blanketing the stretch of ocean ahead of her.

Memories whipped over her like the wind gusting across the cliff top, twining around her with inescapable force. She swallowed back bile. The drug was lowering her defenses, but she wouldn't let it conquer her. She would win, damn it.

Although this sure was cutting it close.

Darcy scanned the dense expanse of trees. She couldn't triumph in a hand-to-hand battle, but maybe she could run. Or find a weapon.

A sinister gleam sparked in Perry's eyes. "That's right, think about fighting."

God, had she been mumbling or was this guy that intuitive? She couldn't waste words on discussion, not when she needed to concentrate her fuzzy senses on finding a way out.

"Please do struggle." Perry inched closer, even swung his gun to the side, then arced it back on her tauntingly. "That will make it more fun. The bruises won't matter when your broken body is recovered at the bottom of the cliff. Or go ahead and try to run. That's fine, too. I like the chase and this is the last one I'll ever have."

Okay, Max. This would be a super time to show up. Fuel reserves were heading into the red with the crash only seconds away. Darcy scanned the trees—

And there he was.

Him.

Max stepped out of the forest, into the clearing, his Glock raised and steady just as the sun broke the horizon. The rising sun gleamed through the bleached tips of his hair, silhouetting him like an avenging angel. She knew the drugs were messing with her perceptions but didn't care right now. Max's strength was such a welcome sight she just wanted to soak up the view. He hadn't made her wait at all.

He'd been two steps ahead of them the whole time. How could she have ever doubted? And if she lived through this, she sure wouldn't question this man's love again.

Max measured the steps between himself and Darcy. Then between Darcy and the edge of the cliff.

Too close. He clicked through the options in his head, a head reeling with relief over finding Darcy still alive. Wobbly but alive. She stared back with glazed eyes as Perry jerked her closer.

Jammed a 9mm in her side.

What had Perry done to her since taking her? He couldn't let himself sink into that nightmare. The past half hour scouring the island had been beyond hell.

And then the answer had exploded into his mind with more of Darcy's Technicolor perceptions. He knew exactly where a sick bastard intent on replaying her past would go. Lovers' Leap, where her kidnapping had culminated before.

The SPs and Crusty were only minutes away from responding to his alert—hopefully hauling ass up the cliff right now.

If Darcy had minutes left.

Max searched her for signs of injury, but her flight suit seemed unmarred by blood. She squeezed her eyes shut, tight, blinked hard and shook her head. Drugged. She'd been drugged and was fighting it. Of course Darcy was fighting. Her slack arms took on a whole new meaning as he realized how hard she must be battling sleep.

Hang on a little longer.

Gun level, Max eased left, closer to the three-sided edge of the cliff. He searched for an opening, a clear shot at Perry that wouldn't put Darcy at risk, and damned well couldn't find more than a small patch of Perry's shoulder right beside Darcy's head. He needed more time. "Perry, I don't know what the hell's going on here, but think of your family. Your wife and your kids. Don't make them live with knowing you're a murderer."

"I'm already a killer, Max." Perry's gun pressed deeper into Darcy's side as he dragged her limp body nearer to the edge. "Every agent overseas I turned in who died. That's already on me. What's one more? It's over and I know it. I am so damned tired of playing second-string Robin to your Batman front and center. I want to take some satisfaction with me."

Satisfaction? What was he missing here? If he could fit that last piece into the puzzle, he would understand how to play this scene out longer and buy time for backup. "Satisfaction? For what?"

"You should have been the one to die that day instead of Eva."

Damn right he should have died in her place, and he would have to live with that for the rest of his life. But he'd never had a clue Perry took her death so hard. Their Agency connections had been minimal.

Whatever Perry had in mind, no way in hell did Max intend to accept a replay of the past today with Darcy.

"That's right, Max. Remember it all. Who do you think Eva cried to every time you disappeared for your next big-guy deep-cover assignment? She respected me, the way I was willing to take on low-level operative status for my family. I did all this for love."

For his family? What kind of twisted logic was that? The guy had sold out his country, turned traitor. That wasn't love for his family.

Love?

Max looked at Perry again and saw... Holy hell, the guy was married.

"Yeah, Max." He nodded, his gun hand wavering. "I loved Eva, too. And you let her die."

Darcy twisted to glare at her captor. "Bastards who sell out agents killed her. Bastards like you."

The full power of Perry's hatred pulsed through the air. Illogical but real. Max didn't need the words to confirm a thing. Perry was through waiting—ready to go over the edge.

With Darcy.

A woman so incredible as she fought like hell to stay awake, holding on to life and giving him any advantage she could. He only had maybe six inches of Perry's chest in sight. Darcy too close.

Her only chance lay in Max taking that shot. And praying she didn't launch over the cliff.

The Glock weighted heavy in his hands. He stared at her one last time. Hoped she would read his intent and prepare. Prayed she would see how much he loved her.

Max cocked his head to the side, aiming. "Perry?"

"Yeah, *boss?*"

Max pulled the trigger.

The bullet tore through Perry's shoulder. Propelled him backward toward the edge, his arm banded around Darcy's waist.

"Max!" she screamed.

No! He launched forward. Darcy flung her arms out, kicked backward as she angled over the side with Perry. Max ran, reached. Her hand clapped against his wrist even as Perry's body dragged her down.

Max's fingers clamped around her forearm, and he wasn't letting go. Ever. He set his feet. Jerked. Perry's crazed eyes met his over Darcy's shoulder for one expanded second.

And then he fell away.

Max yanked Darcy into his arms. He buried her face in his neck to shield her from the vision below and thanked God she wasn't down there, as well.

For once he was grateful for those fast reflexes his power-tripping father had honed in him over the years. "Damn it, you scared the hell out of me."

Her limp arms looped around his neck as streaks of morning sun fingered through the sky. "I guess that means you were worried and you care. But we're gonna have to work on your delivery, Doc."

"We've got time for that." Thank God they had time. He cupped her face and studied her dilated pupils. "Are you okay?"

"Just doped up on some kind of...dolphin drug," she answered, her words slurring as her lids drooped. "Maybe you could take me back to our room and have your wicked way with me. Except I probably couldn't stay awake much longer."

He laughed into her hair. No question, it took more than tranquilizers and a brush with death to down

Darcy. Damn it, yes, he loved this incredible woman. "You're a tough one, Darcy Renshaw."

"Well, like Perry said earlier. I'm one tough lady to kill," she answered just before sagging in Max's arms.

He scooped her up, turning toward the path. They had a long road ahead of them in more ways than one. But none of that mattered anymore. He'd been willing to do anything to keep this incredible woman alive. Now he knew he would do anything to keep her in his arms, as well.

Darcy leaned back in Max's arms and gazed out over the ocean from Lovers' Leap. How much difference a day made in perspective. Standing on the edge, she basked in the noonday sun gleaming off the breakers. The windswept cliff stirred none of the fears she'd felt over the past weeks whenever she''d considered climbing the path. The past had eased its grip.

Thanks to Max.

Wind twined around them in their bathing suits, bound them. Sea-scented air whispered memories of yesterday, softened by the hope for all her tomorrows.

Max's arms locked around her, maybe a bit too tight, but understandable. She recognized the protectiveness for what it was. Love. Fear of losing her. More love.

She liked that "more" best of all.

She didn't intend to pull away, but rather savor this moment with him. There wouldn't be much time for them to talk in person in the coming weeks with Max tying up his investigation. And he planned to fly out to talk to Perry's family.

Max had already made it clear to his superiors that Perry's wife and children never needed to know the details of his traitorous activities. Let them take comfort in believing he had died in the line of duty.

Kat Lowry had finally contacted a JAG. No way would she walk, but she might escape execution for handing over operatives by trading evidence for her life.

Darcy let the wind carry away tension as she watched the tide ripple, Max's dolphins riding those waves into the open sea. He'd set them free hours earlier. Alone. Max would never be a chatty guy, but he was perfect for her.

And of course then he'd invited her to join him now.

So many goodbyes for both of them today. Now if they could just figure out how to hold on to each other.

Max rested his chin on her head. "You know I'm not going to walk away from you when we leave here."

The man's ability to sense her thoughts was getting downright spooky. And wonderful. "I know. We're going to make this relationship work."

He nodded against her.

She squeezed his hands, clasped together over her stomach. "I don't even want to think about going home yet. I miss you already. But I can use leave-time to fly out to California. I'll try to wrangle TDYs to wherever you are." She stared down at their linked hands. Keeping that bond was worth fighting for. "I'll also look into cross-training to another plane with a base closer to you."

Max lifted her hand and pressed a kiss to the inside of her wrist. She tipped her head to glance back and share a smile. She saw the appreciation in his eyes, could also see he understood what it cost her to offer.

Saying goodbye to him forever would cost her too much more.

He dropped their linked hands back to her stomach. "Hold that thought for a while. I've been doing some thinking myself."

Darcy absorbed the heat of his chest through her back. Please, please, please don't offer to go the professor route, a tempting proposition for her. But so very wrong for him.

"I'm going to talk with some people I know in the OSI."

She turned in his arms to face him. "Run that by me again?" She couldn't envision Max in a uniform any more than in the classroom.

He hooked his arms around her back, low. "The switch from CIA to civilian employee in the Air Force OSI wouldn't be a problem."

Like Vinnie.

She let the image shift in her mind. Slowly, it took shape into the man she'd seen standing down Perry just a day earlier. "How would it work?"

"I'd most likely go straight in as a GS 12. My cover as Doc Keagan is shot to hell anyway for CIA ops." His eyes gravitated back out toward the seascape below. "No doubt, the OSI will make use of my diving skills when possible. But I learned something these past weeks thanks to you. It's the investigation that drives me."

The image shifted one last time before settling with total rightness. She could see it, the way he'd blended all the parts of his present, his past, even reconciling baggage with his military father enough to be a part of his world.

Best of all, she also saw her future with this wild, unconventional man who stole her breath and her heart with his moody smiles and tender touch. She could learn a lot from him. Being with Max would keep her horizons broad, her regimented world so very colorful. Only Max could have figured a way to blend their lifestyles.

Max, as an OSI secret-agent dude bringing all that unconventional vision and those colors to the Air Force world.

To her world, as well. Perfect. "You're good, Max. Damned good."

His mouth kicked up in a wicked smile echoed in his eyes.

She slugged his arm. "At your job."

"That, too."

Her fingers unfurled to caress his tattooed bicep along an arm that had saved her. "Thank you for the big rescue."

"Rescue? Hell, woman, I've never met anyone less in need of rescue. I'm sure you'd have bludgeoned him with his tasseled loafers before much longer."

Maybe. Maybe not. "Thank you for coming soon enough so I didn't have to."

He winked. "No problem."

Her fingers twisted in the softness of his over-washed T-shirt. "I hated feeling helpless like all those years before. I hate losing."

"Staying alive, hell, staying awake constituted a major victory. I don't care how precise Perry thought he was with those drugs. He pumped enough tranqs in you to down two dolphins for twelve hours." He bracketed her face in his broad palms. "Darcy, you're a survivor. You were twelve years ago and you are now."

His words soaked into her brain, into her. Damn it, she *was* a survivor. But thanks to Max, she was also alive. Really alive in her soul, ready to take on the world.

No fear. Not because she'd battled and won, but because she finally realized she didn't have to battle alone.

Yes, she could take on the world, fight her own wars, but having a wingman in life as well as in the air was a good thing. A person needed someone to count on. Even more so, somewhere to recharge. Recoup. Simply be alive.

As she was in Max's arms.

Loving Max didn't mean losing herself. She'd just found a better, stronger Darcy in being with him. "Hey, Doc?"

"Yeah?" He toyed with her dog tags draped along the neck of her bathing suit.

"I'm ready now."

She wondered how long it would take him to catch on as he stared back at her.

Not long at all.

A smile creased dimples into that bronzed-god face of his, this man who heard her needs before she voiced them. Sometimes before she even thought them.

Yes, he understood, but he deserved to hear the words.

She skimmed her hands up his arms and around his neck. "Do you know who I am?"

"Yeah, Darcy, I think I do. But why don't you go ahead and tell me, anyway."

"I'm the woman who loves you, damn it." She reinforced her vow with a brush of her lips against his. "And I'm also damned certain I always will."

His laugh caressed her skin seconds before his lips. Max kissed her back. Just kissed her, but man did he ever have a way with just kissing her until she couldn't think.

Finally, she rested her forehead against his and inhaled the scent of coconut oil, musk and man. Hers. "If you start having second thoughts about the OSI, don't do it. I would never ask you to make this change for me."

"I know. That's what makes it so easy." His sea-green eyes lit like the glistening sparks on a cresting breaker. "And the way I see it, Darcy, this is a new adventure. A new wave. Sometimes a guy can get so caught up in catching every wave, he misses the big one."

She looked into his eyes and realized that unspoken communication of his worked both ways. She could see that Max was really okay with the new direction for his life.

For their lives.

She allowed herself the pleasure of finger combing his spiky hair. "No dreadlocks, please."

His laugh rumbled up and free, taking flight into the air and over the ocean he sometimes called home.

"No dreadlocks." He rocked their hips closer, igniting the ever-present spark between them. "Although, I've been thinking about a new tattoo."

That fire kindled hotter. "Oh, really? Where? What?"

"A bird."

"An eagle? Cool."

He shook his head. "I'm thinking more along the lines of a wren." He placed her hand over his heart. "Right here."

Darcy sighed, totally hot and completely melting all at once. "Maybe I should look into a tattoo for myself."

"We won't be the most conventional couple on base."

"What woman needs conventional when she can have pineapples, coconut oil and *more*."

She stretched up into another kiss, tracing the spot along his chest over his heart—a heart that picked up pace under her hand as Max lowered her to the soft pad of grass for a lifetime of more.

Much more…

* * * * *

Look for Crusty's story
coming soon as Catherine Mann's
WINGMEN WARRIORS
series continues.

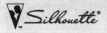

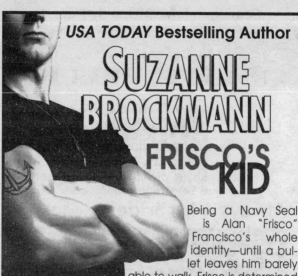

**Like a spent wave,
washing broken shells back to sea,
the clues to a long-ago death had been
caught in the undertow of time...**

Coming in
July 2003

Undertow

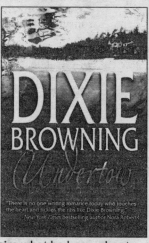

DIXIE
BROWNING
Undertow

"There is no one writing romance today who touches
the heart and tickles the ribs like Dixie Browning."
— *New York Times* bestselling author Nora Roberts

Cold cases were
Gray Hollowell's specialty,
and for a bored detective
on disability, turning over
clues from a twenty-seven-
year-old boating fatality
on exclusive Henry Island
was just the vacation he
needed. Edgar Henry had
paid him cash, given him
the keys to his cottage, told him what he knew about
his wife's death—then up and died. But it wasn't until
Edgar's vulnerable daughter, Mariah, showed up to
scatter Edgar's ashes that Gray felt the pull of her
innocent beauty—and the chill of this cold case.

Only from Silhouette Books!

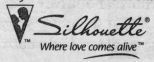

Silhouette®
Where love comes alive™

From *USA TODAY* bestselling author

EMILIE RICHARDS

comes the story of a woman who has played life
by the book, and now the rules have changed.

Faith Bronson, daughter of a prominent Virginia senator and wife
of a charismatic lobbyist, finds her privileged life shattered when
her marriage ends abruptly. Only just beginning to face the lie
she has lived, she finds sanctuary with her two children in a
run-down row house in exclusive Georgetown. This historic
house harbors deep secrets of its own, secrets that force Faith
to confront the deceit that has long defined her.

PROSPECT STREET

"Richards adds to the territory
staked out by such authors as
Barbara Delinsky and Kristin Hannah....
Richards' writing is unpretentious and
effective and her characters burst with
vitality and authenticity."

—*Publishers Weekly*

*Available the first week of June 2003
wherever paperbacks are sold!*

MIRA®

 Silhouette®

COMING NEXT MONTH

#1231 ALWAYS A McBRIDE—Linda Turner
Those Marrying McBrides!
With a false identity and a demand for justice, Taylor McBride set out
to find the father who had abandoned him. Instead he found sweet
Phoebe Chandler. Soon his thirst for revenge was replaced by
a hunger for her. But after all his deception, could she possibly trust
that his love was true?

#1232 SHOOTING STARR—Kathleen Creighton
No one could keep Caitlyn Brown from helping children in
danger. Not the sniper who stalked her, and not C. J. Starr, the man
who'd nearly cost her her last mission. Though he'd fought to make
amends, she couldn't forget his betrayal. But when her stalker finally
found her, could she set her doubts aside and trust C.J. with her life—
and her heart?

#1233 LAST SEEN…—Carla Cassidy
Cherokee Corners
Duty brought Adam Spencer to Cherokee Corners, Oklahoma,
to check on his cousin's widow, Breanna James, and her daughter.
Desire made him stay. Her career as a vice cop had placed her
in danger, and he vowed to keep her safe. But Adam rekindled
a passion Breanna had denied for a long time, and "safe" was
the last thing she felt….

#1234 ON DEAN'S WATCH—Linda Winstead Jones
His assignment was to stake out the former home of a dangerous
convicted criminal, not to fall for said criminal's ex-girlfriend. But
that was exactly what undercover U.S. Marshal Dean Sinclair did
while watching Reva Macklin. As his investigation heated up, so did
their attraction. But would her feelings remain when Dean revealed
his true identity?

#1235 ROSES AFTER MIDNIGHT—
Linda Randall Wisdom
Detective Celeste Bradshaw was looking for Prince Charming, but
this was no fairy tale. She was hunting a rapist and had tracked him to
Luc Dante's restaurant. Luc didn't trust cops, but there was no
doubting his desire for Celeste, and no doubt that he would do
anything to save her when she became the latest target….

#1236 BURNING LOVE—Debra Cowan
A serial arsonist was terrorizing fire investigator Terra August, and
she needed detective Jack Spencer's help to stop him. But the city
wasn't the only thing on fire. Jack and Terra burned for each other,
igniting emotions neither was prepared for. With time running out,
they had to face their feelings, or let their love go up in flames….

SIMCNM0603